WICKED SEAS

A Rowan Gray and Ivy Morgan Mystery

LILY HARPER HART

HarperHart Publications

ONE

Jack Harker tilted his head to the side as he looked at his girlfriend's version of a bathing suit and debated what to say.

"Um ... ."

Ivy Morgan, her brown hair streaked with pink, wrinkled her nose as she fingered the fraying straps on the simple one-piece suit. "I guess I should've thought about this before you surprised me with news of the trip, huh?"

Jack cocked his head to the side. "I don't know. You could start a new trend on the cruise ship. You know ... hobo chic."

Ivy's expression was rueful. "I think I'm stuck with it. We fly out early tomorrow. There's no place in town to get a new bathing suit."

"Yes, well ... ." Jack delicately took the ragged clothing item from her and tossed it in the corner trash bin. "You're not wearing that."

"Then I'm swimming naked. On a cruise ship with thousands of people, that might get uncomfortable."

When Jack surprised Ivy with a vacation a few weeks before — one they both desperately needed after months of drama and danger — she'd been unbelievably excited. It was only after thinking it through that he realized she'd never really been on vacation. She'd never been away from Shadow Lake for more than short jaunts. She'd certainly never been on a cruise ship. When that realization hit hard and strong, Jack decided he was going to make this trip the best it could possibly be for his future bride — a pre-honeymoon honeymoon, if you will — and he was determined to see that through.

"It's a cruise ship, honey. They have bathing suits in the shops located right on the ship."

"They do?" Ivy didn't know why she was surprised. It made sense. Still ... . "They're not like tiny little bikinis that don't have proper coverage for butts, right?"

Love swamped Jack at the oddest of times, but the rush that coursed through him thanks to the worried look on her face was enough to knock him back a step. "They'll have something you like. I promise. The ship we're going on has something like fifteen stores, I think. You'll find something you can live with ... and I will buy it for you as a vacation gift."

"You don't have to do that." Ivy cast a look to the discarded bathing suit. "I wish I would've thought about this sooner. I'm not much of a bathing suit person."

"I noticed." He stroked his hand down her slim back, his lips curving when he sensed the unease pooling between her shoulder blades. "Honey, do you want to tell me what's bugging you?"

The question caught Ivy off guard. "Why do you think something is bugging me?"

"Because we've been together for a year and I'm familiar with your moods. I thought you were looking forward to this trip."

"I am," Ivy said hastily, grabbing his wrist and staring hard into his eyes. "I'm so excited for this trip I don't even know where to start when it comes to packing. It's just ... I've never been on a ship before. I don't know what to pack. I mean ... are my clothes even right?"

Jack wasn't used to Ivy being unsure of herself. Of all the women he'd met throughout his life, she had the best sense of self — a confident but not egotistical way of carrying herself — and her sudden self-doubt was maddening. "Honey, your clothes are fine. All those ankle-length skirts flooding your closet? They're good. You don't have a lot of shorts, but that's fine. Basically you need a bathing suit, a cover-up, and something to wear for dinner each night. That's it."

"Right." Ivy tapped her bottom lip as she surveyed the suitcase they were packing. It was huge, big enough to fit all the items both of them would need, but Ivy was convinced she was going to fill it with the wrong things and that would somehow ruin their trip. "Maybe I should run to Traverse City. They have a twenty-four-hour department store. We should put together a list of things we need."

Jack snagged her by the back of the neck before she could get a full head of steam and lose the packing momentum they'd worked so hard to establish. "No. We have everything we need. We've made lists for two weeks straight — and checked them for two weeks straight — and now we're going to pack. We have to be up in six hours. Frankly, we should've done this earlier."

"I know. It's just ... ." She trailed off when her black cat Nicodemus hopped into the middle of the suitcase and plopped himself down, immediately washing his flank instead of meeting Jack's challenging gaze.

"We're not taking him," Jack interjected the moment Ivy opened her mouth. "I'm not kidding. He is not cruise-friendly. Heck, he's not Jack-friendly." As if to prove his point, Jack reached out a finger and waved it in Nicodemus's face. The cat responded by swatting him hard enough to nick skin.

"Ow." Jack slipped his sore finger into his mouth. "That hurt."

"I like how you messed with him until he reacted and now you're acting as if you're the wounded party," Ivy said dryly, shaking her head. For some reason, Jack's ridiculous relationship with the cat — something that was an everyday occurrence — settled her. "You're right, though. I'm going off the rails. I don't care what people think about my clothes. I never have."

Jack slid her a sidelong look. "That's one of my favorite things about you."

"Yeah, well, it's one of my favorite things about me, too. I have no idea why I'm being like this."

"I do." Jack abandoned his finger ministrations and slung an arm over her shoulders. Ivy was tall for a woman — slim and lovely, too — but Jack still towered over her by several inches. "You've never traveled to a real destination before. You don't know what to do with

3

yourself because you're so excited it's futzing up that busy brain of yours."

"I've traveled before," Ivy countered, her eyes flashing.

"When?"

"My parents took Max and me to the Upper Peninsula camping when we were kids."

Jack fought the urge to laugh ... and lost. "So you drove three hours north and camped for a week? That's not the same thing, honey."

"I know but ... it's not as if I'm some country bumpkin. You don't have to wow me with bright lights and a big city."

"Oh, is that what you think?" Jack tightened his grip on her and pressed a kiss to her forehead. "I know you're not a country bumpkin. I happen to think it's cute how excited you are for the trip. No, I mean it. Ever since I surprised you with it, you've been a mass of moods. Thankfully those moods are kind of adorable."

Instead of immediately responding, Ivy heaved out a sigh. She knew he was right. Her head was all over the place. She'd never been one to lose her mind over simple things ... but here she was losing her mind over a bathing suit.

"What are you thinking?" Jack asked after a beat.

"That I hope they have nice bathing suits on the ship." The smile Ivy graced Jack with was blinding. "What's the name of the ship again?"

"The Bounding Storm."

"That's kind of a neat name."

"I like it, too." Jack's fingers were gentle on the nape of her neck as he worked to lull her. "We have a loft suite. I'm not quite sure what that is, but I've seen photos, and it looks nice."

"I've heard cruise ship rooms are terrible."

"Yes, but this ship is supposed to be top-of-the-line and these suites are significant upgrades."

"And how did you get the upgrade again?"

"I know a guy."

Ivy smirked. "I guess it's better than you knowing a girl."

"There's only one girl in my life." He poked her side before wrapping his arms around her and kissing her cheek. "I happen to love my one girl." His voice was barely a whisper.

"I love you, too. I'm sorry I've been so crazy about this. I can't seem to help myself, though."

"I don't mind that you're crazy." Jack rubbed his hands over her back, the simple motion relaxing her. "I'm thrilled that we can do this together. It's a first for both of us."

"Yeah." Ivy briefly pressed her eyes shut as she rested her ear against his chest. "We still need to pack."

"We do."

"I'm probably going to melt down five more times before we hit the ship."

"I'm well aware."

"I'll be better when we get there."

"Honey, we're going to have so much fun all these packing meltdowns are going to be nothing but a funny story we tell people when making them listen to tall tales about our vacation adventures for years to come."

"That's the plan." Ivy lifted her chin and gave him a quick kiss. "We need to finish packing. Then we need to go to bed so we can get on the road early."

"You mean you need to get to your next meltdown."

"True enough."

"Let's do it." He cupped the back of her head and kissed her hard. "In twenty-four hours, we'll be in our fancy loft suite and looking forward to tropical drinks as we watch the sun set."

"Bring it on."

"There's my girl."

ROWAN GRAY SAT ON THE beach building a sandcastle as her boyfriend Quinn Davenport scoured the security report for their next cruise. The sun had set hours before, but the beach was well lit and Rowan had no trouble seeing through the darkness to design her castle.

"What's tomorrow's cruise entail again?" Rowan asked as she used her fingernail to fashion a turret.

"It's a mix," Quinn replied, his full attention on the packet as he rested his back against a picnic bench. "Half the ship is regular guests — which is a nice break after all the theme cruises we stacked one after the other — and the other half is some political group."

Rowan wrinkled her nose. "Political group? Like a senator or something?"

"No. That would be easier to deal with. It's one of those mission groups who have a cause they're trying to raise awareness about."

"Oh." Understanding washed over Rowan as she used the back of her dirty hand to brush her auburn hair away from her face. "Like ending animal testing or sexual harassment in the workplace, right?"

"Kind of." Quinn lifted his eyes and smirked at her castle. "That one is ... unique. What's with the high tower?"

"That's where we live so we can get away from the hustle and bustle of the rest of the castle."

"That sounds like a good plan."

"I'm full of good plans," Rowan confirmed.

"Hmm." Quinn's attention slid back to the packet. As security chief for The Bounding Storm, it was his job to identify and head off any issues that might cause problems over their upcoming excursion.

Rowan watched him a moment, amused, and then abandoned her castle so she could crawl closer and see what had snagged his attention. Usually when they came to the beach the night before a cruise, he was all about her. This evening, it was almost as if he'd forgotten she was even there.

"Hey." Her voice was low and throaty as she snuggled closer, taking him by surprise. "Do you want me to head back to the ship so you can be alone with your friend?"

"What?" Quinn cocked an eyebrow, confused. "What did you say, sweetheart?" He reluctantly dragged his eyes away from the report and focused on her.

"Oh, I feel so loved," Rowan drawled, teasing. "I asked if you wanted me to leave."

"Why would I want that?"

"Because you're obviously more interested in that report than me."

"That's not true." Quinn slid an arm around Rowan's back and maneuvered her lithe body so she was positioned between his legs. Then he proceeded to turn back to the report. "It's just ... this is weird."

Rowan tried to follow what Quinn was looking at, the light from the parking lot illuminating the pages, but she wasn't sure what the report actually said. "I don't know what this means." She pointed toward the top of the page. "What's the National Organization for Clean Minds and Hearts?"

"A really long name for a group."

"Ha, ha." Rowan made an exaggerated face and poked his side. "I'm serious. I've never heard of that group. Are they a cult?"

Quinn laughed despite himself. "Not a cult ... at least not exactly a cult. That might be more entertaining. It's a coalition that has gained attention thanks to support by several famous individuals — one of whom is married to a senator and another who is married to one of those mega-rich pastors you see on television — and the organizers have started a crusade to clean up the media."

Rowan rested her head against Quinn's chest as she ran the information through her head. "I'm not sure I understand," she admitted after a beat. "How are they going to clean up the media? Are they going to fine newscasters or something?"

"Not *that* media," he chuckled. "I'm talking about movies, books, and television shows. This group wants to limit pornography, violence on television, and fine the creators of any movie with cursing."

It took Rowan a moment to absorb the news. "Huh."

"That's all you have to say?" Quinn was amused. "The queen of the bad horror movie is fine with the idea of blood-free schlock? What are we going to do when a storm hits and you can't reenact Jason Voorhees's camp massacres? Are you telling me you're okay with a gore-free killfest?"

Rowan was appalled. "Of course not. There's no sense watching a horror movie without the gore."

"That's what I thought."

"I guess I don't understand the group," Rowan hedged. "Why would they want to dictate what others can and can't watch?"

"You just don't want them to take your horror movies from you." He kissed the tender spot behind her ear and smiled when she squirmed. "I don't want them taken away either. You get romantic after watching a slasher movie. I have no idea why but ... I'm happy to benefit from your mood."

"Ha, ha." Rowan pinched his knee in a teasing fashion. "How will you like it if the group gets their way and outlaws those movies you like with the fast cars and scantily-clad women?"

"What's offensive about that? And those *Fast and the Furious* movies are classics. You like them as well as me."

"I like Vin Diesel when he's all sweaty," Rowan corrected. "You like Michelle Rodriguez when she's all sweaty. It's a match made in cinema heaven."

Quinn barked out a laugh. "You are adorable."

"I know, but I'm being serious." She tapped the report to draw his attention. "It says right here that they're interested in instituting a modesty clause that includes women in media only being able to wear one-piece bathing suits."

"Well, that's just ludicrous."

"I agree. How do you think that attitude is going to fly on a ship full of women who like wearing string bikinis made of dental floss?"

"Oh." Realization dawned on Quinn as he straightened. "Oh."

"There you go," Rowan smirked. "I'm thinking your job is going to be harder than normal on this one. A group of puritanical media watchers who think sex is evil are going to be taking up shop on our ship. That's bound to go over well."

Quinn scowled. "Crap. I didn't even think about that." He wet his lips, his mind busy. "I should probably have some contingency in place. Maybe we can isolate one of the pools for the group and try to keep the rest of the guests at the other pools."

"I don't know that's fair," Rowan argued. "I mean ... it's not everyone else's fault that these people want to tell them how to dress."

"I get that. I simply want to cut down on potential problems.

What happens when one of those women in the dental floss bikinis gets drunk and decides she doesn't like being judged?"

"That's a good point." Rowan rolled her neck. "I didn't even consider that. We could have brawls at every end of the ship if we're not careful."

"Exactly."

"How are you going to handle that?"

The look Quinn shot Rowan was withering. "I think you mean 'how are *we* going to handle that,' don't you?"

Rowan shook her head, her lips curving. "I'm the ship's photographer. Security isn't my concern. That's my big, strong boyfriend's job."

"Ha, ha."

Quinn ruthlessly tickled her as she squealed, his security report forgotten as they grappled in the sand.

"Stop," Rowan gasped, tears streaming down her eyes from the laughter. "It's not my fault you're the smartest man on the ship. You're also the most charming man out there. I guarantee you'll have these people eating out of the palm of your hand before you know it."

"Oh, really?" Quinn cocked a dubious eyebrow. "What makes you think that?"

"Because you never wear dental floss despite how fetching I think you would look in it ... especially the flavored kind that would make you minty fresh."

"That did it." Quinn abandoned the report — he could read it in the morning, after all — and focused on his girlfriend. "You'd better prepare yourself, missy. I'm going to break a whole bunch of rules that the National Organization for Clean Minds and Hearts wouldn't like."

"Finally, you're doing something worth doing."

Quinn's grin was wide and lopsided. "Prepare to be amazed."

"I'm always prepared."

"That's only one of the things I love about you."

TWO

"Wow. It looks like a floating city."

Ivy didn't want to be referred to as a country bumpkin, but that's how she felt as she walked hand-in-hand with Jack up the gangway to the ship the next afternoon. Their plane left Michigan long before dawn, landing in Florida three hours later. That gave them enough time to eat and catch a cab to the ship.

Jack smiled as he studied her profile. She looked awestruck, which was something he rarely witnessed. In fact, since meeting her, he could count on one hand the number of times she appeared to be out of her element. Heck, when they went camping, he was the one left scrambling to catch up with her. "Do you like it?"

"How could I not like it?" Her eyes sparkled as she shifted them to him. "I don't even know what to think about it. We have some big ships in Lake Michigan, but this is unbelievable."

"Those are freighter ships."

"And some tourist ships."

"Yeah. This is an ocean liner."

"Well ... it's amazing."

Jack squeezed her hand, pleased at the way her smile never slipped as they closed in on the check-in point. "Okay, I figured we would get the keys to our room, unpack, and then hit the deck for a coconut-flavored drink."

"Cool."

It took them twenty minutes to wind their way to the front desk on The Bounding Storm. The woman who stood behind the desk was young, and the smile she flashed was friendly and engaging.

"Welcome to The Bounding Storm. What name is your reservation under?"

"Jack Harker." He spelled his name as he ran his hand up and down Ivy's back. For her part, she seemed interested in the woman to their left who was trying to wrangle four kids in front of a huge backdrop of a waterfall so she could take a photo.

"Oh, I see you're one of our VIP couples," the woman commented, her smile growing wider. "How great. That means you get special wristbands that allow you to access the private pool at the aft of the ship. No children are allowed there and drinks are served poolside. You also have options for the upscale dining rooms. If you need a reservation at any of our smaller restaurants, simply call the concierge and he will set that up for you."

Jack smiled as he signed the sheet of paper she placed in front of him, handing the wristbands to Ivy as he gripped the handle of the suitcase. "Which way?"

"You have a semi-private elevator that will take you to your rooms." The girl pointed. "Please let us know if we can do anything to make your stay better."

"I think our stay is going to be perfect. Don't you, honey?"

"Hmm." Ivy stirred from her close study of the pretty woman taking photographs. She wasn't sure when she lost track of the conversation, but she was surprised when Jack asked her a direct question and she had no idea what he was talking about.

"Are you drunk already?" he teased, following her gaze. "Oh, I get it."

"You get what?"

"You want your photograph taken. I believe that's part of the package, right?"

The clerk nodded. "Absolutely. Rowan is the main photographer onboard and she does a wonderful job. In addition to the photo taken when you check in, she will also load various action snapshots into a portal for you to peruse if you want to order additional prints after your stay with us. All the instructions are in the packet I gave you."

"That sounds like a plan." Jack tugged the suitcase and inclined his head in Rowan's direction. "Come on. Let's get a photo."

Ivy's eyes widened. "You want a photograph?"

"Why wouldn't I want a photograph? I have the prettiest woman on the ship. I want to make sure I have something to frame to prove that."

"I ... ." Whatever Ivy was going to say died on her lips as she fell into step with Jack. He was determined, and even though she thought it was a bit schmaltzy, she wasn't opposed to a professional photograph. "I wish I didn't have plane hair."

"You're beautiful no matter what." Jack smiled indulgently as the photographer gestured for them to step in front of the backdrop.

"Hi. I'm Rowan Gray. I'm the ship photographer. Can I have your names?"

"Jack Harker and Ivy Morgan."

"Okay. I see you're VIP clients. That means you get your own personal photo portal," Rowan explained. "There will be instructions in your packet on how to access it."

"Great."

"Leave your luggage right here and move to the center of the backdrop," Rowan instructed, her eyes briefly locking with Ivy's. They stared at each other for a long beat, neither of them saying anything.

"Is something wrong?" Jack asked when he realized both women had fallen silent, instantly alert.

"No," Ivy replied quickly, shaking her head. "It's just ... I feel like I know you."

"It's weird that you mention it," Rowan hedged. "I feel like I know you, too. In fact ... where did you go to high school?"

"Shadow Lake High School. It's this really small town in northern Lower Michigan. Nobody has ever heard of it."

Rowan's eyes widened. "I have. I grew up in St. Clair Shores."

"I grew up in St. Clair Shores, too," Jack offered. "That's weird. Which high school did you go to?"

"Lakeview."

"I went to South Lake."

"Small world." Rowan's eyes were back on Ivy. "I've been to Shadow Lake. It was a long time ago. I was a teenager. My father took me there after my mother died because there was some sort of festival he thought I would be interested in."

"We always have festivals," Ivy supplied. "I mean ... always. Like every freaking week."

Rowan chuckled. "I wonder if we ever met. Did you go to the festivals?"

"I usually worked the festivals."

"I guess maybe you seem familiar because you're from Michigan." Rowan's smile widened as she lifted her camera. "It's like having a small bit of home visit."

"Yes, well, we're happy to be visiting you." Jack slid his arm around Ivy's waist and tugged her to his side. "We're looking forward to a fun trip."

"I hope you get everything you're looking for." Rowan took five photos in rapid succession and pulled back to check her handiwork in the viewfinder. "You guys are very photogenic. I'll have the photos up later tonight for you to look at them. If you don't like what you see, call me and we can set up a time for you to take another."

"Oh, don't worry about that," Jack said. "I think we'll be happy with whatever you have. Now, come on, honey. I'm dying to see this room. It's supposed to be spectacular."

"You got one of the loft rooms, right?" Rowan smiled knowingly. "Trust me. Compared to a standard room, they're absolutely fabulous. I didn't even know they were a thing until a few weeks ago and now I've become obsessed with them. I've only seen photos. They try to hide them away from the workers."

"Then I'm definitely looking forward to seeing it." Ivy offered Rowan a half-wave. "Maybe we'll see you later. We can trade stories about growing up in Michigan."

"Definitely." Rowan bobbed her head as she turned to the next woman in line. "Name?"

"Margaret Adkins."

"Okay. Step up to the backdrop and let's see what we've got."

IVY WAS ON PINS AND needles as she waited for Jack to open their suite door. When she stepped inside, she was flabbergasted by what she saw.

"What the ... ?"

"Wow." Even Jack was impressed. "My sister sent me photos, but they didn't do this place justice. Will you look at that?" He gestured toward the loft bed. It was located up a flight of stairs and the wall separating it from the balcony was glass. On the main floor, they had a small living room and office area.

Ivy was utterly flummoxed. "Jack, how did you afford this?" She swallowed hard. "This isn't a normal room."

"No," Jack agreed, sliding his eyes to her pretty face. "It's not normal, honey. As for affording it ... I know someone."

"Jack." Ivy was exasperated. "How?"

He ran his tongue over his teeth. "I sold the house in St. Clair Shores," he said after a beat.

"I know. That's how you helped with the cottage expansion. That's hardly news."

"I made a little more than I expected," he hedged. "It's a seller's market. The guy I sold it to happens to be a real estate agent. I threw in the furniture for free ... and his wife was so thrilled he arranged this as a gift. Apparently he knows one of the bigwigs who works for the cruise liner."

"Wow." Ivy merely shook her head as she stared at the room. "How many rooms are there like this on one of these ships?"

"Not many. That's why I was so excited when he offered it."

"It's amazing." Ivy's eyes were glassy when she turned to him. "This is really amazing, Jack."

"Oh, come here, honey." He opened his arms so she could step between them and accept his hug. "This is only the beginning."

"Oh, yeah?"

He nodded, solemn. "How badly do you want to go upstairs and test that bed with me?"

Ivy fought the urge to laugh but ultimately gave in. "You're going to be a sex machine all vacation, aren't you?"

"You have no idea."

Ivy was already squealing when he started chasing her toward the stairs.

ROWAN WAS TIRED WHEN she finished her shift, making her way to the tiki bar on the main deck so she could indulge herself with some iced tea and her computer as she loaded the photos for sorting.

"Hey, girlfriend," Demarcus Johnson teased in an exaggerated tone as he joined her in the shade. He knew what she wanted before she even ordered and had a huge glass ready for delivery. "You look a little worse for wear. Are those 'no swearing in television' people giving you a hard time?"

Rowan snorted, legitimately amused. "They are a little different," she conceded, glancing around to make sure no one was listening. "One couple actually got in a fight because the wife was convinced the husband was looking at another guest's bare legs. She said this was why they had to join the group in the first place and he was a complete and total pervert because Hollywood made him that way."

Demarcus snorted as he sank into the chair across from Rowan. "That is ... I don't even know what to say to that."

"I don't either," Rowan admitted, her eyes glazing over as the photos uploaded at a rapid pace. "The regular guests seem fine this go-around. I even met a couple from Michigan. They're from Shadow Lake now, but the man grew up in the same city I did. I kind of want to talk to them later."

"Oh, are you getting nostalgic for Michigan? That sounds normal when you live in a tropical paradise."

"Ha, ha." Rowan rolled her eyes. "It's not that I'm nostalgic. It's just ... they're kind of a touchstone. I know it's weird, but I like the idea that we're from the same state. Sue me."

"Oh, chill out." Demarcus waved off Rowan's attitude. "There's no reason to get crazy. I get it."

"They're one of the VIP couples, too."

"Oh, the chick with pink hair?" Demarcus brightened considerably. "Half the staff is talking about her. They think she looks like some Bohemian princess. People noticed her on the deck when she was checking in."

"Who is a Bohemian princess?" Quinn asked, sliding into the chair next to Rowan and leaning forward so he could give her a kiss on the cheek. "How was your day, dear?"

Rowan chuckled. "That's a little domestic, isn't it?"

"I'm trying it on for size. As far as endearments go, it's kind of lame. I'm hoping it makes you want to deliver my slippers to me while wearing a French maid's uniform later."

Rowan's smile slipped. "That is never going to happen."

"Never say never." Quinn winked before shifting his eyes to Demarcus. "Who is the Bohemian princess you're talking about?"

"I don't know her name," Demarcus replied. "She's staying in one of the VIP suites, though. The room is registered under her boyfriend's name."

"Fiancé," Rowan automatically corrected. "He's her fiancé."

Demarcus arched an eyebrow, surprised. "How do you know that?"

"Because I took their photo and she's wearing a ring." Rowan scanned through the photos until she found the ones that depicted Ivy and Jack, tilting her computer screen so Quinn could see the couple in question. "See. She has a diamond on her left ring finger."

"And he looks sloppy in love," Quinn noted, smirking. "I can see why people are calling her a Bohemian princess. She's wearing a long skirt in the middle of a heatwave ...and it looks as if it should be in the display window at a head shop. The hair is kind of odd, too."

"I like her hair." Rowan made a face. "It fits her personality."

"Okay." Quinn widened his eyes at her biting tone. "Did I miss something? I was just commenting on the hair, not insulting her or anything."

"Rowan feels a kinship with the Bohemian queen because she's from Michigan," Demarcus explained. "We were talking about that right before you showed up. Apparently Rowan grew up in the same town as the guy who happens to be boinking the Bohemian lovely."

"Stop calling her Bohemian," Rowan snapped. "She's perfectly nice."

"Do you know the guy?" Quinn asked, curious.

"No. I don't think I ever met him. We lived in the same city but went to different high schools. I think we're close to the same age, but that doesn't necessarily mean anything. I do remember Shadow Lake, though. That's the place my father took me after my mother died. He thought I needed time away from people, and Shadow Lake is pretty much in the middle of nowhere."

"Well, that's kind of interesting," Quinn said finally. "I think it's kind of cute that you feel the need to stand up for her simply because she's from Michigan."

"That's not the only reason," Rowan hedged. "I just ... there was something about her. I felt as if I knew her or something."

"Really?" Quinn discarded his teasing tone. "I don't know what to make of that. Do you think you've met her before?"

"I have no idea. I do plan on talking to her later, though. I don't care how much fun you guys make of me for it."

"I don't think it's a bad idea. She looks interesting." Quinn moved his fingers to the mousepad and moved to the next photograph. "They look happy, huh?"

"They *are* happy. You can feel it practically radiating off of them."

"Do I need to work on my happiness radiation skills?"

"Oh, geez." Demarcus rolled his eyes and got to his feet. "On that note, I'm going to leave you guys to worship one another. If you get any good dirt on your new friends, tell me. I bet she's got an awesome story. If you guys are going to spend all night saying 'no, you're prettier,' then I'm out."

"Oh, speaking of queens," Rowan teased, grinning when Demarcus shot her a look before moving across the bar to take care of some guests. She was still smiling when she turned back to Quinn and found him watching her with questioning eyes. "What?"

"Nothing." He held up his hands in a placating manner. "I'm simply confused as to why you're so interested in this woman. I mean ... she doesn't look like a normal cruise guest. She does have a Bohemian flair, no matter what you say. You seem a little protective of her, though. How come?"

Rowan shrugged, unsure how to answer. "She kind of reminds me of myself."

Quinn's eyebrows winged up. "How?"

"I don't know. When I first came here, this ship seemed larger than life. I didn't think I was going to fit in. Not ever. The way she looked at the lobby, it reminded me of the way I looked at the lobby that first day. She's out of her element ... and really excited."

"That seems like a very specific observation."

"Yeah, well, I have awesome observation skills. In fact ... ." Rowan completely forgot what she was about to say as she flipped to the next photograph in the lineup and focused on the woman in line behind Ivy Morgan. She couldn't remember her name, but the symbol showing in the corner of the photograph was familiar enough to send shivers down her spine. "Quinn."

"What?" Quinn was still smiling, still enjoying messing with his girlfriend, when he turned to the computer. His lips turned down the moment he recognized the symbol — he'd been dating Rowan long enough for her to explain her ability to him — and he glanced around the deck to make sure no one could overhear them before asking the obvious question. "Do you know who that is?"

"Yeah." She checked her notes with shaking hands. "Her name is Margaret Adkins. She didn't say much, was a little grumpy. I didn't exactly engage with her because it was right after Ivy and Jack went through. I was more interested in them."

"Yeah, well, that's why you have me to provide information." Quinn whipped out his phone and typed the woman's name into a search portal. "Oh, well, crap."

"What's wrong?" Rowan's eyes widened. "She's not already dead, is she? I've never seen the omen work that fast."

"I don't know either way if she's dead. I'm guessing not, but I'll check in a few minutes. That's not what I was 'oh, crap-ing' about."

"Do I even want to know?"

"She's with the political group."

Rowan sighed, resigned. "Of course she is. We should've seen that coming."

"Yeah, well, that's going to make getting close to her more difficult. That group is pretty insulated as far as I can tell."

"We still have to try."

Quinn squeezed her hand. "Of course we have to try. I'm going to track her down right now. We'll go from there."

THREE

J ack changed into shorts and a polo shirt to walk the deck with Ivy as they prepared to set sail. Once they christened their room, he was anxious to take a tour. He'd done more traveling than Ivy, but even he was new to the cruise liner experience.

"This is kind of neat, huh?" He picked a lounger close to the railing and patted the spot between his legs so Ivy could get comfortable.

She offered up zero complaints as she settled, smiling as Jack wrapped his arms around her and staring at the shoreline as the boat moved out to sea. The view was spectacular, the sun high in the sky, and her thoughts were as sunny as the bright light bathing them in warmth. "Do you smell that?"

Jack nuzzled closer, the romance of earlier lingering in a manner that made him feel unbelievably relaxed. "I do. You smell like ... summer."

Ivy made an exaggerated face. "Not *that* ... although you're even schmaltzier than normal."

"I don't care. We're on vacation. If I can't be schmaltzy on vacation, what's the point of leaving home?"

"Fair enough." Ivy rested her head against Jack's chest. "I was talking about the ocean air, though. It smells ... salty."

"That's because it's salt water."

"I know that."

"I was simply pointing it out."

"It just ... feels different. I don't know how to explain it. Like it's a special gift because I don't have to work. For days I don't have to work. I don't think I've fully wrapped my head around that."

Curious despite himself, Jack cocked an eyebrow and tilted his head as he studied her strong profile. "Have you ever had a vacation, honey? Like ... taken actual time off work."

"Of course."

She said it too quickly. Jack was instantly suspicious. "When?"

"I've been on lots of vacations. Just this past winter I was on a sort of vacation because the nursery was closed."

Ivy's nursery was her pride and joy, a business she built from scratch. It was located on the backside of her property, and the hardest part about convincing her to join him on vacation had been promising that her father would be more than happy to run the business while she took a week off.

"You didn't take off any time over the winter."

"I did so."

"You did not." Jack refused to back down. "You made lotions and soaps all winter, that lip balm your brother loved so much he threatened to eat it."

"That's more of a hobby than anything else."

"You sell the stuff. You could make a full-time living off that business if you wanted. Just because you tend to limit your time playing cosmetologist, that doesn't mean you didn't work."

"Well, that's not the only time I've taken a vacation," Ivy countered. "Last summer I was off work for days."

"When?"

"Um ... you know when."

Jack knew exactly what time period she was referring to. "You mean when you got shot?"

"I thought we weren't going to bring up that ugly time again. Let's not go there. We're on vacation."

"Uh-huh." Jack rolled his eyes but he couldn't stop himself from chuckling. "I'm right. You've never taken time off from work. This trip is even more important than I thought. You need a break."

Ivy heaved out a long-suffering sigh that Jack recognized as her form of capitulation. "Fine. Just for you, I'll embrace this ... break." She was silent for a beat. "What should we do first?"

Jack snorted. He should've seen it coming. She was on vacation, but she was a curious soul. She needed to see everything, touch everything. Since he loved her, he would deny her nothing. "How about we walk around the ship, take a look at everything on the deck, and then get a drink at that tiki bar we saw on our way outside?"

Ivy nodded, happy. "I want something with an umbrella in it."

"That sounds like a plan."

"I HAVE SOME INFORMATION about Margaret Adkins," Quinn announced as he joined Rowan on the deck. She was making a big show of taking photographs — from a distance — but she'd kept close to Margaret for the past two hours and she showed no signs of letting up.

"Lay it on me," Rowan said, snapping three photos in rapid succession.

Quinn arched an eyebrow and shook his head. She was a master at multitasking. "She's one of the founding members of the National Organization for Clean Minds and Hearts."

"Still a stupid name for a group."

"Totally, but I've delved a little deeper into the group. In fact, I messaged Fred to see if he could find anything good. He sent back some preliminary stuff and promises to get more as soon as he can sit down and start pulling records."

Fred Delmore and Quinn served overseas in the military together and they were unbelievably close. Rowan only recently met him, but she was a big fan of the gregarious private investigator. "He probably got good stuff ... and made snarky comments while delivering it."

"See, you already know him." Quinn winked. "Okay, there were three founding members of the society. I refuse to call it by its full name. Margaret was one. Joseph Guthrie was another. Brenda Farmer was the third. They were all members of the same church, a South Carolina Baptist church located in Folly Beach."

"Where's Folly Beach?"

"It's on the coast. It's cool. If we ever get a chance, we'll take a week and head up there. The pier is amazing and the food is to die for. They have a crab shack where they lower a bucket right in the center of the table so you have someplace to keep your discarded shells."

A seafood lover at heart, Rowan brightened considerably. "That sounds amazing."

"I thought you might like that." Quinn's grin was lightning fast before he sobered and focused on the printout he brought to the deck with him. "About three years ago, they formed the group after a high-profile murder in Charleston. A high school boy claimed video games made him kill his parents. He was found mentally impaired and sent to a hospital rather than a prison."

"That sounds like a terrible case, but I'm not sure that warrants falling off the rails."

"I'm guessing there's more to the story than that, but that's what they're spouting whenever they can find someone to conduct an interview. That case supposedly made them realize that movies, books, television, and music were to blame for many of the ills of the world, including what happened to this kid. They say he wasn't mentally ill as much as driven to insanity by some video game he was playing."

"What video game?"

"I don't know. Some shoot 'em up thing. I don't have that information."

"Okay. Continue." Rowan snapped another photo of Margaret and checked to see if the symbol remained.

"Is she still in danger?" Quinn asked, recognizing the way her lips curved down.

"Yeah."

"Well, we'll figure it out." He hoped he sounded more convinced than he felt. "So, three years ago the three of them started this group. They recruited locally in Charleston and then carried their message out to other states. Now, apparently, the group has more than a hundred thousand members, including the celebrities I mentioned earlier."

"And how many members are on this cruise?"

"You're a smart girl. I already checked. There are just under a thousand members of the group booked on this trip."

"That's not necessarily a great turnout."

"No, but traveling isn't cheap. It's not just paying for a room on the ship, but travel to Florida, food, tips, and island ports."

"Good point." Rowan lowered her camera and leaned against the railing. "I guess I'm confused. What would be the motive to kill this woman? Sure, I don't get the point of blaming media for what others do, but she's hardly the first to hold this opinion."

"No, but she is getting louder and louder," Quinn said. "In fact, she's been trying to hobnob with politicians in an effort to get more press coverage for her cause."

"It's kind of ironic that she wants more television time even though she believes television is evil, huh?"

"Yeah. I was kind of thinking the same thing." Quinn flipped to the second page of his small report. "All three of the founders are on this cruise. I'm not sure what the others look like because we've been focused on Margaret. Do you think you can find them in your photos so we can make sure they're not in danger, too?"

"I don't mind double-checking, but I went through all the photos already. She was the only one with the omen."

Quinn pursed his lips. "Well, there goes that theory."

"What theory was that?"

"I thought maybe someone thought the trip might be a good way to get rid of the group's leaders. If the other two are safe, though, that doesn't exactly give me hope that I'm on the right track."

"It doesn't mean that you're wrong," Rowan offered. "Maybe Margaret is simply the first to die."

"I wish we knew more about why you see these omens, and exactly what they mean."

"Maybe we'll learn more from my father." The second the statement was out of her mouth, Rowan wanted to backtrack. "Or maybe he doesn't know either."

Quinn bit back a sigh. The return of Rowan's father — a man thought to be dead — had been a cloud hanging over them since he showed up on the ship recently. They'd talked about his return, and the fact that he was technically in hiding since, but Rowan was still struggling with the information he provided during his visit. "Do you want to talk about that?"

Rowan immediately started shaking her head. "No. I'm kind of sorry I brought it up."

"Fair enough. You can have as much time as you want to process things. I have no interest in pushing you."

"Thank you." Rowan meant it. "When I'm ready, you'll be the first to know."

"That sounds like a plan." Quinn turned back to the sheet of paper. "I don't know what to do other than watch her."

Rowan held her hands palms out and shrugged. "So ... let's watch her. Maybe we'll get lucky and her enemy will show his face right away."

"That would be a nice change of pace."

IVY'S DRINK WAS SO big it almost obliterated her entire face. The bartender, a friendly guy with a wide smile, was so amused at the length of time it took Ivy to decide on a drink he finally chose one for her. It was blue and Ivy was already tipsy even though she'd only imbibed half of it.

"This is the best thing ever," she enthused, grinning as Jack directed her toward a small table. "Seriously. We should make these at home."

Jack's smile was indulgent. "If you want to get drunk and show me your blue tongue at home, I'm all for it."

Triggered by the suggestion, Ivy extended her tongue and laughed.

"Very nice." Jack leaned forward and smacked a loud kiss against her lips. "You're in a very playful mood."

Ivy lowered her voice. "I don't want to alarm you, but I think I might be drunk."

He snorted so hard he coughed. "Oh, honey, I think you might be, too. We probably should've eaten lunch before I started plying you with alcohol."

"Probably," Ivy readily agreed, taking another big sip of her drink. "Too late now."

Jack rested his hand on hers to get her full attention. "I'm only letting you drink the one. Then you're getting some water and food."

"You're no fun."

"I don't want you wasting your first vacation on a never-ending hangover."

"I guess that's fair." Ivy leaned back in her chair and rested her bare feet on Jack's ankles.

Concerned, Jack glanced under the table. "You didn't lose your shoes, did you?"

Ivy was solemn. "Maybe."

Thankfully, her flip-flops were under the table. She had a habit of running around barefoot at home. In fact, the first time they met she was barefoot ... even though she'd just discovered a body in the ditch and was forced to spend the next few hours in the middle of a crime scene.

"We should've bought sandals with straps so you couldn't just slip them off and leave them somewhere. Ah, well, it's not the end of the world. If we need to buy shoes, we'll buy those, too."

"We still haven't picked out a bathing suit."

"We? I wasn't aware that I was allowed to help you choose. Now that I know that, I'm thinking something pink, like your hair."

Ivy made a face. "I'm thinking something blue like ... ." She extended her tongue.

"Oh, I'm never going to let you live this down." Jack was all smiles as he reclined in his chair, his gaze tracking to Rowan as she cut her way across the deck. She looked distracted, harried even, but she managed a friendly wave for a few workers when they called out to her.

"Hey, you guys." Rowan looked surprised when she realized she was almost standing on top of Jack and Ivy. "How is the Michigan contingent enjoying the trip so far?"

"We're having a good time," Jack replied lazily. "My fiancée is drunk ... and maybe a little hormonally worked up."

Rowan snickered as she glanced under the table to where Ivy was rubbing her feet against Jack's sandals. "I see. At least she's having fun, right?"

"Definitely."

Something occurred to Rowan and she thought it best to warn Jack and Ivy, just to be on the safe side. "Um ... it's not really my place to talk out of turn about the guests, but you might want to avoid the National Organization for Clean Minds and Hearts."

Jack's face was blank. "I'm not sure what that means."

"It's a political group," Rowan explained. "There's a large contingent of them on the ship. They're ... interesting."

"Now I'm officially intrigued."

"Me, too," Ivy said, reaching for her glass.

Jack snagged it from her before she could take another drink. "Honey, maybe you should hold off until I get some food in you, huh? We'll get lunch downstairs and then hit the stores so you can pick out a bathing suit. I'm afraid if you finish this I'm going to have to put you to bed."

"You've never complained about that before."

"It's not even two yet."

Ivy sighed but acquiesced. "Fine. I am a little buzzed."

"It's because you barely drink at home." Jack turned back to Rowan. "Sorry about that. What were you telling us about the group?"

"Oh, I don't know that it's important, but I don't want your trip ruined or anything," Rowan explained. "They're a militant family values group. They're convinced that violence in video games and sexually suggestive lyrics make people do bad things. We've been reading about them on the internet — you know, just to get a feeling on whether they're going to be trouble — and apparently they think sex outside of marriage is a bad thing. Like ... a really bad thing."

"I think she's suggesting we look like we have sex outside of marriage," Ivy noted, causing Jack to smirk.

"We're engaged," Jack pointed out. "We're getting married this summer ... although someone still hasn't picked a date."

Ivy scowled. "I'm working on it."

"Work faster."

"I don't know that it matters to them," Rowan said. "I've only been a member of the crew for a few months and this is the first time I've come across a group like this. Everyone else seems to think it's funny — so maybe I'm overreacting — but they make me nervous."

"I don't like puritans either," Ivy offered. "I'm a big proponent of living your life however you want as long as you don't hurt others."

"I agree." Rowan bobbed her head. "I can't shake the feeling that these folks are the sort who would've stoned witches to death back in Salem, or burned them at the stake in Europe. I don't know why I feel that way, but they're starting to make me nervous."

Jack and Ivy exchanged a weighted look that wasn't lost on Rowan.

"Did I say something wrong?" The photographer asked nervously, shifting from one foot to the other.

"No." Jack shook his head. "We're fine. Thank you for telling us. We'll do our best to avoid the group. We're just here to have a nice, relaxing time. We've already started."

Ivy pushed out her blue tongue again. "Yup. I'm totally relaxed."

Jack extended his hand as he stood, helping Ivy to her feet and waiting patiently as she slipped back into her shoes. "I doubt we're going to be their type of people. We plan on sticking to each other, eating a lot of good food, swimming, and dancing. That's as heavy as we're going to take things."

"You should go to the main dining room tonight," Rowan suggested. "They have crab legs ... and they're to die for."

"That sounds good to me."

"Not me," Ivy countered. "I'm a vegetarian. I didn't think about that. I wonder if I will be able to find anything to eat."

"Oh, don't worry about that," Rowan said hurriedly. "There are plenty of vegetarian options. Although ... how can you go through life without crab legs?"

"Surprisingly it's never been an issue."

"If you say so." Rowan gave them a wave and then returned to her trek across the deck. "Have fun. Don't drink too many blue cocktails."

Jack linked his fingers with Ivy's and gave her a little tug to point her in the right direction. "That's the plan," he said. "I'm sure we'll see you around."

"I'm sure you will, too."

4

FOUR

Ivy dressed in one of her normal skirts for dinner, an ankle-length tie-dyed offering that set off her eyes. Jack found the ensemble charming, but Ivy gave herself a critical eye in the mirror.

"I should've brought different clothes."

"Why?" Jack asked as he stretched out on the bed and stared at the ceiling. "I think you look cute."

"You always think I look cute."

"No, I always think you look beautiful," he corrected.

Ivy shot him an exaggerated look. "That was ... sadly charming."

Jack snickered as he propped himself on his elbow and studied her. She had a bit of color to her face, although she was militant about the sunblock once they secured a bathing suit for her and hit the pool. Her smile was ready, her eyes twinkling and engaged, and she seemed somehow lighter.

"You *are* beautiful," he pressed, grinning. "You're also no longer drunk. I kind of miss blue-tongued Ivy." He rolled to a sitting position and snagged her around the waist so he could tug her to the bed. Even though their suite was larger than anything he could've imagined, there wasn't a lot of extra space around the bed, so his task was easy.

"Stop." Ivy slapped at his hands and laughed. "You're going to mess up my hair."

"I don't care." Jack rolled so he could pin her and stare hard into her blue eyes. Their shopping trip earlier had proven enlightening — mostly because she was convinced he wanted her to wear a skimpy bikini and she wouldn't allow him to lodge an opinion on her choice — and their afternoon had been lazy as they lounged by the pool. Jack couldn't remember a more relaxing afternoon. He was feeling calm and snuggly ... an interesting combination that made his hands roam over her as he pressed a kiss to her mouth. "I love you."

Ivy widened her eyes as she stopped mock wrestling with him and grabbed the sides of his face with her hands. "You're in lust."

Amused despite himself, Jack cocked an eyebrow. "Excuse me?"

"You're in lust," she repeated, refusing to back down. "All you can think about is sex."

"All I can think about is you."

"It's the same thing."

"No, I'm thinking about all kinds of things right now and only twenty-five percent of them revolve around sex. That's positively prurient."

"I don't think those 'save the children from bad movies and television' people are going to feel that way."

Jack momentarily sobered. "Yeah, that is the only down side of our trip," he admitted, rolling to his back and carrying her with him so he could settle her slim frame on top of his muscled chest. "I wish I'd known they were going to be here. I would've picked a different week."

"They haven't been terrible," Ivy countered. "I thought they were kind of funny when they yelled at that couple playing volleyball in the pool."

"Yes, there's nothing I like more than a good 'you're a sexual deviant' diatribe. I'm simply glad it wasn't pointed at me."

"I feel lucky, too." Ivy's smile was sly as she looked down at his face. "I say we just ignore them. They seem caught up in their own little world ...and they're all wearing those little badges. If we see them, we'll head someplace else. Besides, didn't the girl behind the front desk say we have access to some VIP pool if we want? I doubt they'll be hanging there."

"That, honey, is a very good idea." He kissed the tip of her nose. "As for another good idea, we should head to dinner. I'm starving." As if on cue, his stomach growled, causing Ivy to giggle.

"I'm hungry, too. Let's eat." She laughed as Jack grabbed her around the waist, hoisted her up and proceeded to carry her across the bedroom and toward the stairs. "I can walk by myself."

"It's your vacation. I want to treat you like a princess."

"Princesses walk by themselves."

"Not my princess."

"Oh, geez." Ivy rolled her eyes as they hit the main floor. "You're really full of yourself today, aren't you?"

"It's only going to get worse, honey. Wait until I force you to dance."

"Oh, man."

"Yeah, yeah, yeah."

ROWAN MET QUINN IN front of the dining room, her camera still hanging around her neck. She'd spent a long afternoon shadowing Margaret Adkins — which meant hours having to listen to members of her group spout absolute nonsense — and she was at her limit.

"Anything?"

Quinn gently combed her hair into place, taking time to slip some of the wild strands that had blown in different directions thanks to a strong afternoon wind behind her ear. "She's alive ... and in the dining room."

Rowan made a face. "That wasn't what I was going for."

"I know. I don't know what you want me to say. I've kept an eye on her all afternoon ... and it wasn't exactly fun for me."

Rowan recognized the tone and quickly corrected her bad attitude. "I'm sorry. I didn't mean to jump all over you. It's just ... I'm antsy. I don't know how to explain it."

Quinn opted to take a practical approach. "Well, there's no reason to get worked up. This isn't the first time this has happened to us. It won't be the last. We'll get through it."

Rowan blinked several times in rapid succession. "Is that supposed to make me feel better?"

"I was hoping it would."

"Well, it doesn't."

Quinn narrowed his eyes. "Hey, I'm trying to help. I get that you're upset, but taking it out on me doesn't do anyone any good. If you want to fight ... maybe we should eat separately this evening. I don't think I can take a fight on top of everything else."

Rowan was instantly contrite. "I'm sorry. I didn't mean to blow up. It's not your fault. It's just ... something happened."

"What?"

Rowan glanced around to see if anyone was listening. Because several guests were too close for her comfort, she grabbed Quinn's hand and dragged him to a corner that was set far away from everybody else. "I was going through my photos before dinner," she explained, grabbing the camera so she could skim through the photos she took over the afternoon. "I think I found something."

"Another potential target?" Quinn was unnaturally calm as he accepted the camera and stared at the photo she showed him. He recognized the couple. The Bohemian pink princess Demarcus was getting such a kick about and her tall and observant boyfriend. He saw them on the deck together this afternoon. They didn't seem the troublesome sort. They were completely wrapped up in each other and ignored the rest of the world. "This is the couple you met from Michigan, right?"

Rowan nodded, miserable. "I talked to them again this afternoon. They're normal. They're on a vacation and having a good time."

"She has pink hair. I don't know that I would call that normal."

"Her hair is cool ... and she's in love with her fiancé. Even more, he's totally devoted to her and they're having so much fun. They're the reason I took this job. Well, not specifically them. People like them, though. This is a big adventure and they're enjoying a once-in-a-lifetime vacation."

"Okay. Calm down, Queen of the Romance Novel." Quinn's eyes

flashed. "What's the problem? I don't see the omen in this photo. They're fine."

"Not *the* omen," Rowan agreed, her heart rate picking up a notch. She'd only noticed the new detail moments before while skimming through photos and she was still flustered by the discovery. "Look in the left-hand corner, though."

Quinn did as instructed, his lips curving down when the hint of a shadow assailed his eyes. He had to look twice, but it was definitely there. "What is that?"

"I have no idea. I've never seen it before."

Quinn blew up the photo so he could magnify the shadow. "This might be a trick of the light."

"Oh, really?" Rowan snagged back the camera and searched until she found another photo. "That's from early this afternoon."

Quinn pursed his lips as he studied the photograph. It was taken on the main deck. The couple in question were sharing a lounge chair, resting and smiling, and the new symbol was clearly visible in the left-hand corner of the shot. "Do you recognize the symbol?"

"No. I'm going to have Sally look at it after dinner, though. She seems to know more about these symbols than we do."

"Yeah." Quinn turned away from the camera as he rolled his neck. "We don't know that symbol means anything bad," he said finally. "It could be something else entirely."

"Like what?"

"I don't know. We do know what the symbol in Margaret's photo means. We've seen that enough times to know that she's in real trouble."

"What are we going to do about that?" Rowan asked, legitimately curious. "We can't follow her every second of the day."

"No. We can make sure to get her back to her room safely this evening, though. I've already assigned a security team to ensure it happens."

"What did you tell them?"

"That we were worried someone didn't like the group's message, thus making her a target. They know to lay low and not draw attention to themselves. I don't know what else to do."

"There's nothing you can do." Rowan was frustrated as she rubbed her forehead. "I'm sorry for being so cranky. It's just ... another new symbol? I spent the bulk of my life thinking there was only the one symbol. It still freaked me out when I saw it, but I'd learned to accept it and move forward.

"Now, over the course of a few months, I'm suddenly up to three symbols," she continued. "We're still not a hundred percent sure what the last one means. I don't know if I can deal with a third."

"You can." Quinn drew her close and hugged her tight. "We're going to figure this out. Don't freak out."

"I'm not sure I can do anything but freak out."

"I'm sure." He was calm. "We're going to work together and figure this out."

"Okay."

He stroked the back of her head. "Do you know what you need?"

"To stop seeing symbols?"

Quinn chuckled. "I was thinking crab legs."

Rowan brightened considerably. "Oh, good idea. I forgot about the crab legs."

"Luckily you have me to remember."

"Luckily I have you ... period."

"Right back at you, sweetie." He gave her a soft kiss before resting his forehead against hers. "I swear we're going to figure this out. Don't let things get to you."

"I'll do my very best."

"That's all I ask."

IVY WAS PLEASANTLY SURPRISED by the vegetarian offerings and found plenty of items to fill her plate. She was far more amused, however, by the fact that Jack found enough to fill two plates and he was pulling off an interesting balancing act as he directed her toward a small table set away from most of the guests.

"Are you planning on me rolling you back to the room?" Ivy asked.

"I'm not ruling it out." Jack glanced around. "Where do you think the drinks are?"

As if on cue, a waitress appeared at the edge of the table. "Do you need something to drink?"

Ivy smothered a laugh at Jack's surprised expression and nodded. "I would like an iced tea, please."

"I'll have the same," Jack said, waiting until the waitress departed to sit and fix his fiancée with a pointed stare. "What are you laughing at?"

"I don't think I've ever seen you eat that much," Ivy replied, unfolding her napkin and placing it on her lap. "You've got a fairly healthy appetite but this is ... wow."

"Hey, they have prime rib and crab legs. This is like my happy place."

"And I thought I was your happy place," Ivy teased.

"You are definitely my happy place. Today, tomorrow, and forever. I ... hey, where are you going?"

Ivy was back on her feet. "I want some rolls. I'll be right back."

"You stay there. I'll get them."

"You don't have to wait on me."

"You're on vacation. I want to wait on you."

Ivy sighed, charmed despite herself. "I keep thinking this is going to get old ... but it hasn't yet."

"Enjoy it." Jack winked as he turned and headed back to the buffet table. He had to wait for an opening in the line to grab Ivy's rolls, but a tall man in a blue shirt and tan shorts held up his hand to allow Jack to cut in front of him.

"Are you sure?" Jack hedged. "I just need to grab some rolls."

"Go ahead," the man replied, smiling. "You're one of the VIP guests, I believe. That means you can cut in front of anyone."

"I don't think that's necessary." Jack placed several rolls on a plate and fixed the other man which a curious look. "How did you know I was a VIP guest?"

"Quinn Davenport." He introduced himself with a head bob and jutted out his hand. "I'm head of security."

"Oh." Jack shook his extended hand. "It's nice to meet you. I wondered about the security on this ship. It has to be difficult to patrol."

"We don't have too many problems," Quinn said. "Occasionally we have an overzealous guest or two. Nine times out of ten, though, that's caused by alcohol and as soon as the guest sleeps it off, everything is back to normal."

"I can see that." Jack gave Quinn a long look. "You don't look like the sort of guy who would run security on a cruise ship."

Amused despite himself, Quinn arched a speculative eyebrow. "What is a cruise ship security chief supposed to look like?"

Jack inclined his chin toward a man across the way. "Him."

Quinn followed his gaze and frowned when he realized he was looking at a member of his own staff. It was one of the guards he assigned to watch Margaret, in fact. "How did you know he was one of mine?"

"It's not hard to tell. I'm a trained observer."

"Oh, yeah?" Quinn fancied himself an observer of sorts, too. "You're a cop, aren't you?"

The question caught Jack off guard. "How did you know that?"

"Let's just say I'm a trained observer, too."

Intrigued, Jack gave Quinn another long look. "You have a military background."

Quinn smirked. "Apparently we're both trained observers."

"Apparently."

Since he was interested in getting more information about Jack and his fiancée — figuring out the new symbol was important to Rowan — Quinn decided to prolong the conversation. "You're from Michigan, right?"

Jack couldn't hide his surprise. "How did you know that? Is this because we're VIP guests?"

"I should probably say yes and let you think we're that proficient at customer service, but my girlfriend told me."

"Your girlfriend?"

"Rowan. She's the photographer. She seems enamored with your girlfriend."

Jack glanced over his shoulder to where Ivy sat, her attention fixed on her food. "Oh. That makes sense. I think they're going to chat about living in Michigan before the trip is over. Rowan seems keen to talk about it, although from where I'm standing, she moved to a much better climate."

Quinn chuckled. "Home is still home. She said you grew up in the same city, although she doesn't know you."

"St. Clair Shores is fairly large. We went to different high schools."

"Ah, well, it's still neat." Quinn hoped he was coming off as friendly rather than invasive. "Is this a special occasion for you guys? I mean ... any reason behind the vacation."

"My sister managed to help me arrange it. I simply wanted to get Ivy away from work for a week or so. She owns her own business and the spring, summer, and fall are her busy months."

"What does she do?"

"She owns a plant nursery."

Try as he might, Quinn couldn't think of a single reason a plant nursery would incite someone to violence. Of course, he had no idea what the symbol meant so there was always a chance Ivy wasn't in danger after all. "Well, that sounds like a lot of work."

"You have no idea. I thought being a cop was difficult. She works a lot harder than me."

"I think the hours are probably long for both. Still, I'm glad you're having a good time. If you need anything, don't hesitate to ask."

"I'll do that." Jack carried the rolls back to the table and chuckled when he realized Ivy was halfway done with her dinner. "And I thought I was the hungry one."

"You were gone a long time," Ivy noted as she took the plate from him. "Who was that guy you were talking to?"

"Ah ... Quinn. He's head of security."

Ivy straightened. "Is something wrong?"

"No, Little Miss Worrywart. He was simply asking if we needed anything. He's involved with the photographer. He asked about being from Michigan. That's what took so long. He's also ex-military."

"It seems you guys had quite the conversation."

"Yes, it's a bromance for the ages," Jack teased. "He's a nice enough guy. I think it's part of his job to keep a watch over things. It's probably exciting to live on a cruise ship, but it's not all fun and games. He's responsible for a lot of people."

"I like the idea of a vacation on a ship. I'm not sure I would be okay living on one."

"That's because you're a nature girl. You love digging in the dirt ... and running through the forest ... and hanging out in your fairy ring. I bet there's no mushroom hunting on The Bounding Storm."

Ivy mock shuddered. "Well, then we definitely can't live here."

"I'm fine living in Shadow Lake. This, however, is a nice vacation."

"Definitely."

"Eat your dinner," Jack prodded as he sawed into his prime rib. "Once we're stuffed full of expensive food, I see dancing in our future."

"I didn't realize you were such a slave to music."

"I simply like dancing with you. Is that a crime?"

Ivy shook her head. "We can dance ... although a moonlit stroll on the deck sounds nice, too."

"I think we can manage both of those."

Ivy's smile widened to the point where it threatened to overtake her delicate features. "I'm really starting to like being on vacation."

"That makes two of us."

FIVE

Quinn woke to an urgent call on his cell phone. It was still early — he thought he had another hour to snuggle with Rowan — but the insistent beeping of his phone told him otherwise.

"Hello." He was barely awake when he uttered the greeting.

"What's wrong," Rowan murmured, curling closer to him.

He didn't answer, instead stroking her back as he tried to lull her back to sleep. There was no reason for her to be up early.

Quinn listened to the other end of the conversation, which included a lot of babbling, for a full minute. When he found his voice, his instincts took over and he snapped into action. "I'll be there in ten minutes. Don't let anyone in that room ... and don't let the other guests know what's going on. We don't want to create a panic if we can help it."

When he disconnected, he found Rowan wide awake and staring at him. "What's going on?" she asked, her voice scratchy.

"Margaret Adkins is dead." Quinn knew better than lying, or dragging things out. He offered up the statement in a matter-of-fact manner. "It looks like she was strangled."

Rowan bolted to a sitting position, horrified. "But ... how? You had men watching her."

"I had men follow her to make sure she made it back to her room last night," Quinn clarified. "They weren't there all night."

"Why?"

"Because I couldn't justify it."

Rowan didn't want to come off as accusatory but she couldn't stop herself. "If they'd stayed, she might not be dead."

"Yes, well ... it is what it is." Quinn refused to get into an argument so early in the morning. "I'm sorry."

Rowan was instantly contrite. "I didn't mean to blame you. That's not fair. I'm sorry."

"It's okay." He pressed a kiss to her forehead. "I should've forced them to stay overnight. I thought it would be okay once she was locked in her room."

"We should get dressed and head down there."

"I should get dressed and head down there," he corrected. "There's no reason for you to have to see this."

"I need to see it. I can't help you figure it out if I don't see it. Besides, I used to be a photographer for a newspaper. I guarantee I've seen worse."

Quinn didn't like it, but he acknowledged that was probably true. "We need to be quick. Once word of this gets out, we're probably going to have a nightmare on our hands thanks to the other members of that group."

"Then let's go."

"WHAT DO YOU THINK is going on there?" Jack stood at the corner of the hallway as he and Ivy left for breakfast, his eyes on a group of people outside a guest's room, activity bubbling and bustling. He couldn't see inside, but it was obvious there was a lot of action happening beyond the door.

Ivy shifted closer to Jack so she could peer around his tall frame. "I don't know. Maybe someone got drunk and got in a fight."

That was possible, but Jack felt a different vibe. "I think it's something bigger than that."

Ivy raised an amused eyebrow. "Oh, really?"

"Yes, really." Jack tapped the end of her nose. "Call it a hunch."

"It's that cop intuition of yours." Ivy pressed her hand to Jack's chest and smirked when she realized his heart was pounding a little faster than normal. "You're just dying to see what's happening in that room, aren't you?"

Jack shook his head. "No."

"I don't believe you."

"Well, that's on you."

Ivy tugged on her patience and reminded herself that Jack was the one who arranged for the special vacation. He was essentially her knight in shining armor this week, which meant he deserved a little leeway. "If you want to hang around and see what they're doing, that's certainly your prerogative. I'm starving, though. All that dancing last night worked up an appetite. I need breakfast. You can stay here while I eat if you want, though. I'll swing back around when I'm done stuffing my face."

Jack snorted. "Yeah, right. That sounds exactly like something I would do."

Ivy lowered her voice. "I'm not the only one on vacation. You're on vacation, too. You don't have to be a police officer today."

Her earnest expression tugged at Jack's heartstrings. "You're absolutely right. Today I'm your fiancé. Let's get something to eat and then decide what we're going to do with our day."

"Are you sure?"

Jack nodded. "I just want you."

ROWAN WAS FAMILIAR ENOUGH with Quinn's working style that she knew to hang back as he surveyed the scene.

Margaret Adkins was in the middle of the bed, what looked to be pantyhose tied around her neck. Her eyes were open and unseeing, and she was fully dressed.

"I don't think this was a sexual assault," Quinn said as he circled the bed with one of his most trusted aides, Mark Dexter. "All of her clothes look intact."

"That's the outfit she was wearing in the dining hall last night," Rowan offered helpfully. "I remember because the pink suit reminded me of Pepto-Bismol."

"Yeah. I remember the suit, too." Jack snapped on a pair of rubber gloves and lifted Margaret's hand so he could get a look at her fingernails. "I'm not sure if she got a piece of her attacker, but make sure that scrapings are taken all the same. It might be important."

Dexter nodded. "Of course."

"How did you find her?" Rowan asked, her curiosity getting the better of her. Quinn hated it when she overtook investigations, but her natural busybody nature wouldn't allow her to remain silent. "I mean ... who reported her death to you?"

"That would be her assistant," Dexter replied, his eyes scanning the small notebook in his hand. "Her name is Emily Little."

"We're going to need to talk to her," Quinn said as he knelt close to Margaret's head. "Do you know where she's at right now?"

"We segregated her in her room," Dexter explained. "I left Andrew with her so she wouldn't be alone. We didn't want her telling stories out of turn before we could get direction from you, though."

"That was smart." Quinn rolled his neck. "I'm not the doctor, but I think she's been dead about six hours based on lividity. That puts her death around two this morning."

"What about the cameras?" Rowan asked. "Were they in operation?"

"Yes and no," Quinn answered. "The group bigwigs — I think there were about twelve of them, including assistants and helpers — got a block of rooms together. They claimed they didn't want the cameras close to their rooms to be operational because they're against technology, yada, yada, yada."

Rowan pursed her lips. "Something tells me you don't believe that."

"I don't believe it in the least." Quinn opted for honesty. "I think they were worried that there might be some shenanigans going on and didn't want to risk their actions being caught on camera."

"Shenanigans?" Rowan was understandably confused. "What do you mean?"

"He means drinking ... and maybe a little carousing," Dexter supplied. "Perhaps a few people going into each other's rooms and not leaving until morning."

Rowan's mouth dropped open. "Oh, *those* types of shenanigans."

Her reaction was enough to remind Quinn of exactly why he fell in love with her. "You're so cute sometimes," he muttered under his breath, earning an annoyed look from Dexter. "What? Don't tell me you didn't think that was cute."

"I would never tell you anything of the sort," Dexter replied without hesitation. "If I did, you would smack me around and fire me."

"I would never fire you for thinking she's cute. I might smack you around."

"Yes, sir." Dexter didn't have much of a sense of a humor, but he nodded perfunctorily.

"Well, we need to get the medical staff in here," Quinn said finally. The Bounding Storm didn't have a medical examiner — it was unnecessary — but the on-staff doctor could perform an autopsy. "I want some answers. It's probably best to get the body out of here before things get busy in an hour, too."

"I'll handle it," Dexter said. "Where are you going?"

"I need to question the woman who found her. What did you say her name was again?"

"Emily Little."

"Yeah. What room is she in?"

EMILY LITTLE WASN'T WHAT Rowan expected. Quinn allowed his girlfriend to tag along for questioning, but only if she promised to keep her mouth shut. As always, Rowan made the promise even though she occasionally forgot her mouth had a mind of its own.

"Is Margaret dead?" Emily asked, her eyes red and puffy as she sat on her bed. She was young — barely twenty-two, if Rowan had to guess — and she looked as if she wasn't yet mature enough to deal with emotional upheaval.

"She is," Quinn confirmed, adopting a sympathetic expression. "I'm sorry for your loss."

"Oh, this is just the worst." Emily made a wailing sound as she threw her forearm over her eyes and started sobbing. The display was weird enough to cause Rowan and Quinn to exchange a dubious look before Quinn cleared his throat and barreled forward.

"We need to discuss a few things with you, Miss Little."

"You can call me Emily." The young woman batted her eyelashes to clear the tears as she focused on Quinn. Rowan couldn't be certain, but there was something flirtatious about her attitude. It was overt enough that it grated. Rowan wisely kept her mouth shut ... for now.

"Okay, Emily." Quinn kept his smile in place. "What were you doing in Mrs. Adkins's room this morning? I mean ... why were you there?"

"I'm her assistant."

"I understand that, but you let yourself in the room."

"Oh, are you asking why I have a keycard? Margaret wanted it that way. I'm supposed to do certain things for her — like making sure her clothes are steamed for the day — and she doesn't like to be bothered when she's taking a nap or doing something else. Sometimes she needs to meditate to clear her mind and she doesn't like it when I knock and interrupt her. She gave me one of her room keys."

"Okay." To Quinn, that sounded a bit ridiculous. It wasn't his place to judge. "Why were you there this morning specifically?"

"To make sure her outfit was ready."

"She had a special outfit for the day? I wasn't aware you guys had any planned events ... other than a few meetings in the ballroom later in the week."

"We didn't have planned events, but Margaret is the face of the group," Emily explained. "It's a very important group. It's going to change the world one day. Although ... I wonder if that will still happen now that Margaret is gone. She was the one who did all the work. You know, fighting the good fight."

Rowan thought that sounded like a rehearsed line, something Margaret forced Emily to say when witnesses were around. Whether Emily believed it was up for debate.

"So Mrs. Adkins simply wanted you to make sure her outfit was ready for the day?"

"I have a list of duties I have to perform each morning," Emily replied. "That includes getting Margaret's outfit ready, helping curl her hair and applying her makeup, and following her around to make sure she gets everything she needs for breakfast.

"Then I get an hour break before I have to bring her a mid-morning snack and take notes while she talks to various people," she continued. "Margaret got her best ideas when talking to others."

"So, basically you're saying that she took other people's ideas and pretended they were her own," Rowan interjected, earning a warning look from Quinn, which she proceeded to ignore. "That's what it sounds like to me."

"That's not what I'm saying," Emily shot back, her voice turning shrill. "I don't even know who you are. Who are you?"

"Ms. Gray is part of our investigative team," Quinn supplied smoothly. "I'm sure she didn't mean to insult your memory of Mrs. Adkins."

Rowan was certain that's exactly what she intended to do, but she saw no reason to make things worse. "Yes. I'm sorry."

"I need you to tell me what you saw when you let yourself into her room, Emily," Quinn prodded, gentle. "It's important. Did you touch anything? Did you move anything?"

"Oh ... um ... ." Emily tapped her bottom lip. "It's all such a blur. Everything was normal when I first opened the door. I remembered thinking it was weird that the lights were still out — Margaret was an early riser, she said it was a holdover from when her husband was alive — but I flipped on the lights and that's when I saw her."

"Did you touch her?"

"No." Emily shook her head. "I know that probably sounds awful. Most other people would've tried to give her mouth-to-mouth or something. I could tell she was dead, though. I didn't touch her. I ran in the hallway and there was a room service boy walking in my direction so I asked him for help."

"Okay." Quinn kept his face smooth and placid. "That makes a lot of sense. Did Mrs. Adkins have any enemies that you're aware of?"

"Oh, no. Everyone loved Margaret."

"She never got any threats? That doesn't make a lot of sense to me given what she does for a living. Since she's trying to infringe on how some people raise their families, I would think that leads to a natural amount of animosity."

"Oh, you didn't say threats. You asked if she had enemies. Enemies are different than threats."

Quinn didn't see how. "Okay. What kind of threats did she get?"

"Oh, she got all kinds. I was responsible for running her public email and you wouldn't believe the messages she would get. They were vile. People would tell her she needed to ... have sex." Emily lowered her voice for the last part of the sentence. "They would give suggestive ways for her to have to sex with herself. They said she should stop worrying about what other people were doing and start worrying about herself."

"That sounds awful." Quinn swallowed the mad urge to laugh. He couldn't believe how naive Emily came across. She was either one of the slowest people he'd ever met or Margaret Adkins had groomed her to be purposely obtuse. He wasn't sure which option made more sense. "Can you remember any specific threats?"

"Well, there was one man who said he was going to chop her up into little bits. He lived in Colorado, though, and when the cops tracked him down they claimed he was thirteen and not a threat."

"I see." Quinn pressed his lips together to keep from laughing. Technically it wasn't funny, but Emily's delivery was so flat that he almost felt as if he was trapped in a comedy show. "Did he at least get a warning?"

"Yes, and his parents took away his video games. Margaret said that his threat was proof that what she was saying was true."

"I can see that. Anyone else?"

"Um ... Artemis Butler."

Quinn was thrown for a loop. "The movie director?"

"Margaret said his movies were so foul she was going after them first and he supposedly said he was going to kill her before she had a chance to go after his life's work."

"Did you actually hear him utter a threat?"

Emily shook her head, solemn. "No. But Margaret talked to him and said it was real. She tried to get the cops involved, but they declined. Margaret said it was because he was famous, but she had every intention of pursuing him until she got her way."

"That sounds like a great lead." Quinn tugged a notebook from his pocket and clicked his pen. "I'm going to need a list of everyone you can think of. Even if it seems like it's probably a dead end, I want you to give me all the names. Do you think you can do that?"

"Absolutely. I want to help. Margaret was like a mother to me."

"Well, we're going to do our very best to figure out who did this. I promise you that."

AN HOUR LATER, QUINN FELT wiped as he left the room. Rowan had remained silent for the bulk of the list-making session, but the handful of eye rolls Quinn caught told him his girlfriend was having none of it.

"I take it you don't believe that Morgan Devane was purposely plotting Margaret Adkins's death," Quinn said as he pressed the elevator call button.

"You mean the Morgan Devane who has won four Oscars? Yeah, I don't think she cared about Margaret Adkins."

"I don't think she did either."

"And yet you have a list of a hundred celebrities that supposedly wanted to hurt Margaret. That seems a little out there."

"Yeah." Quinn absently rubbed the back of his neck as they stepped into the elevator. "I'm starting to think that Margaret talked big, lied every chance she got, and purposely picked a naive assistant who would automatically believe her."

Instead of agreeing, Rowan snorted. "Oh, don't kid yourself. She's smarter than she pretends to be."

"How do you figure?"

"She spent the whole time checking you out."

"That simply means she has hormones, not brains. Besides, if she was smart, she would've picked up on the rather obvious clues that I'm very taken."

"She was still checking you out," Rowan pressed. "Since she's part of a group that seems to be fine dictating everyone's family values, I can't help but wonder if that's a natural impulse she's supposed to be keeping under wraps."

"I'm more interested in why the group was so insistent about the cameras," Quinn admitted. "I mean ... was there really that much bumping and grinding going on behind closed doors?"

Rowan giggled, legitimately amused. "I guess we're going to have to find out, huh?"

"Yeah, because the other option is even worse."

"What's the other option?"

"That someone in Margaret's inner circle decided ahead of time that they were going to kill her and turning off the cameras was a preemptive move to cover up for a murder."

Rowan hadn't even considered that. "How are you going to find out?"

"I am going to find out who made the request and go from there."

SIX

Jack and Ivy were in the dining room when Quinn and Rowan arrived. Since she felt helpless for falling down on the job where Margaret was concerned, Rowan decided she wasn't about to let that happen to Ivy.

"Where are you going?" Quinn asked when she set off in the opposite direction of their normal table.

"We're not eating alone this morning."

Quinn looked beyond her, to where she was headed, and sighed. "This isn't your fault, sweetheart," he said as he scurried to catch up with her. "There's nothing you could've done to save Margaret."

Rowan wasn't convinced that was true. "Why even have this gift if I can't use it to save people? It's not really a gift if there's nothing good about it, is there?"

"I think everything about you is a gift."

"Oh, geez." Rowan rolled her eyes and slowed her pace. "That was a really sweet thing to say but now isn't the time. I'm feeling a lot of rage, and it's difficult to hold onto that rage when you're being Mr. Perfect."

Despite himself, Quinn smiled. "Well, I happen to like being perfect."

"And I happen to like that, too. I'm angry, though. Not at you or even myself. I guess I'm angry at the world."

Quinn let loose an exaggerated sigh. "And you're going to make up for it by making sure nothing happens to the Bohemian princess, huh?"

"Don't call her that. I like her."

"Fine." Quinn recognized this was an argument he couldn't win so he decided to capitulate. "I'm going to help you because that's what Mr. Perfect does. I don't want you getting manic about this."

"What have I ever gotten manic about?"

"You don't really want me to answer that, do you?"

Rowan narrowed her eyes. "You don't have to eat with us if you don't want to, but I'm getting to know them better. I think, if I get to know them and find out if they have any enemies, that means I'll have a better shot at figuring out what that symbol on the photograph means."

"I have no problem eating with them. I met Jack last night. He seems like the friendly sort. I haven't yet met her, but you clearly like her. I just want to point out before this goes too far, though, that you've made an assumption that she's the one in the photo the symbol is pointing to. Each photo you showed me featured both of them."

Rowan was taken aback. "Huh. I didn't even think about that. You're right. I naturally assumed it was her."

"I'm not saying you're wrong," Quinn said hurriedly. "I've learned to trust your instincts. I'm simply curious why you're assuming it's her."

Rowan had no answer for him. "I don't know."

"Well, just keep it in mind when we're eating with them. He might very well be the source."

"Fair enough."

"YOU'RE REALLY PIGGING out on that bacon, huh?" Ivy noted as she cut into her blueberry pancakes and eyed the pile of meat on Jack's plate with overt curiosity.

Jack shrugged, noncommittal. "I'm sensing a cop joke hidden somewhere in there."

"I don't really make cop jokes."

"Fair enough." He bit into a slice of bacon and evenly met her gaze. "Do you have a problem with me eating bacon?"

"No. I've simply never seen you eat that much."

"That's because we don't keep it at the house. We usually have eggs and hash browns for breakfast, occasionally pancakes and waffles. We don't ever have breakfast meats. Why do you think Max will only eat breakfast with us at the diner?" he asked, referring to Ivy's boisterous brother.

"I never really thought about it." She tilted her head to the side, considering. "I should probably keep more meat in the house for you, huh? I make you eat vegetarian at least three times a week."

"You don't make me do anything."

"If there's nothing else to eat, I kind of do force it on you."

Jack let loose an exasperated sigh. "I hate it when you decide to give serious thought to relationship issues that aren't really issues."

"For example?"

"For example, meat. If I wanted more meat, I would simply buy more meat. I know where the grocery store is. I happen to like your vegetarian entrees."

"You liked that dragon fruit dish I made last week?"

Jack involuntarily shuddered at the memory. "Okay, not that particular meal. That tasted like ... a white kiwi with sugar thrown on top."

Ivy chuckled at the description. "It wasn't very good. Even I thought it was gross."

"I love your vegetarian lasagna, though. You make great vegetarian pasta. I do not like those meat substitute patties you keep in the freezer, though. I accidentally thought one of those was a chicken patty a couple of months ago. That was the worst chicken sandwich I ever had."

"You can't taste the difference."

"Anyone with taste buds can taste the difference."

"I think you're exaggerating."

"And I think I'm going to eat my weight in bacon while we're here," Jack countered, popping another slice of bacon into his mouth as Ivy laughed.

Rowan and Quinn picked that moment to approach. Rowan almost felt like an intruder because it was obvious the couple was enjoying each other's company. They were on vacation, seemingly the only two people in their corner of the world. That didn't change the fact that Rowan was convinced the symbol appeared for a reason. She wanted to make sure that reason wouldn't spell disaster for the happy couple.

"Hey." Rowan offered an enthusiastic greeting to announce their arrival. "Do you mind if we join you? I have a hankering to hear about Michigan and Quinn never believes me when I tell him the Coney dog is the state sandwich."

If Quinn was surprised by Rowan's statement, he didn't show it. Instead he merely smiled indulgently and took the seat Jack gestured toward when he nodded it was fine to join them. "I've never understood mixing mustard and chili."

"I love chili dogs," Ivy enthused. "I also love mustard ... and chili ... and onions. They're even better when you throw in some jalapeño peppers."

Jack cast her a pointed look. "You don't eat chili dogs."

"I do so."

"You do not. You're a vegetarian."

"They make vegetarian hot dogs."

"So ... is that like a cucumber on a hot dog bun?" Quinn asked, confused.

Jack found the joke amusing, but Rowan and Ivy rolled their eyes in unison.

"Men," Rowan muttered, shaking her head. "I don't like hot dogs either."

"They really do make vegetarian hot dogs," Ivy said as she slathered butter on a fresh pancake. "I happen to like them. I make a really good vegetarian chili. It's so good."

"Your chili is amazing," Jack agreed. "I don't care how cute you are, though, you're never going to convince me to eat a vegetarian hot dog."

"I'm kind of confused about vegetarianism," Quinn admitted, cutting into a sausage link. "Does that mean you don't eat chicken and fish?"

"Nothing with a face," Ivy replied.

"What about dairy products?" Rowan asked.

"I'm a vegetarian, not a vegan. I happen to like butter, milk, eggs, and cheese as much as the next person."

"That is one good thing about your eating habits," Jack agreed. "If we had to live in a world without pizza, I'm not sure our relationship could survive."

"Ha, ha." Ivy shook her head when he offered her half the doughnut he snagged from the buffet table. "Do you want me to make a joke about cops and doughnuts?"

"If you have a funny one."

Since she didn't, Ivy merely took the doughnut and shoved it in her mouth.

Quinn decided to take advantage of the momentary conversation lull. "Are you a police officer in the Detroit area?"

"No." Jack scratched an invisible itch on the side of his nose. "I used to be, though."

"Really?" Quinn missed the obvious signs that Jack wasn't thrilled at the possibility of discussing his time with the Detroit police force. "That must have been interesting. There's a lot of crime in Detroit, right?"

Jack shrugged. "Actually, Flint has a higher murder rate than Detroit these days."

"I heard that," Rowan said. "Flint has been in the news a lot because of the water crisis."

"Yeah, I think residents in that area have it rough," Jack agreed. "Thankfully, I left the big city behind and moved to Shadow Lake. We don't have crime issues in Shadow Lake ... at least not a lot of them."

"And what is Shadow Lake like?" Quinn was a city boy at heart, so when Jack started describing the town to him, he almost fell off his chair. "One stoplight?"

Jack chuckled, genuinely amused. "That's what I thought when I moved there. Now I kind of like it."

"I think you just like what you found there," Quinn countered, gesturing toward Ivy. "I assume you're a country girl at heart."

Ivy nodded without hesitation. "Definitely. I grew up in Shadow Lake. I can't ever imagine moving unless ... well, I guess if Jack decides he needs a bigger city to work in after we're married, we would have no choice. He hasn't mentioned that, though."

"That's because I don't want to go back to the city," Jack supplied. "I'm perfectly happy in Shadow Lake. I don't miss the city at all."

"You must miss the action," Quinn pressed.

"No." Jack was firm. "I don't miss it."

"Not even a little?"

Jack heaved out a sigh. "I was shot several times in the chest while on the job in Detroit. I almost died. That's when I moved to Shadow Lake ... and I'm not sorry."

Quinn felt like a jerk. "I'm sorry. That was none of my business. I didn't mean to push you that way."

Jack waved off the apology. "It's okay. You didn't know."

Rowan risked a glance at Ivy and recognized the concern on the pretty woman's features. It seemed Jack's past weighed heavily on her, like it did on him. Maybe that was the source of the symbol, Rowan rationalized. Maybe Jack was supposed to die and, because he survived, he was somehow marked. That could explain a few things.

Still, the scenario didn't fit. Even though she was loath to admit it to Quinn, she still believed the symbol was stalking Ivy, not her fiancé. Now, if only she could figure out why.

"You said you grew up in Shadow Lake," Rowan noted. "I'm trying to remember a little about that area. I was young when I went up there with my father, but I seem to remember a Native American reservation up there. Is that right?"

Ivy nodded. "It's actually closer to Traverse City."

"Do you get to spend time on the reservation?"

"My mother, who is something of a Bohemian hippie, took me there when I was a kid," Ivy replied, missing the warning look Rowan shot Quinn at the word "Bohemian."

"What was it like?" Rowan asked, her natural curiosity coming out to play. "Is it like you see on television?"

"Um ... not really. A lot of the homes were run down, but they'd just opened up a new casino and I heard my mother talking to one of the women who lived there and they had high hopes for an economic turn-around. My mother took me there because they had bazaars on the weekends where they sold art and jewelry. She's always been a big fan of stuff like that."

"We should head out there one weekend," Jack suggested. "We're always looking for new stuff to do."

"We could," Ivy agreed. "They have a trout farm and everything. You might actually be able to catch some fish if you go there because they can't get away."

Jack scowled. "I've caught fish before."

"I've never seen you catch fish."

"I throw them back because we live in a vegetarian household."

"Oh, whatever." Ivy was enjoying herself. "You have steak with my brother at least twice a week when the weather is good and I even made you chicken for Christmas."

Jack smiled at the memory. "You did. I had a whole chicken to myself. It was awesome."

Quinn snickered at the moony look on Jack's face. "I never really thought about it before, but you must jump at the chance to eat real food every chance you get."

Jack sobered. "Ivy makes real food. She's an amazing cook. She's only ever made a few things I don't like. There was this dragon fruit thing a few weeks ago. Oh, and then there's the never-ending parade of morel dishes in the spring. I could do without those."

Quinn furrowed his brow. "What are morels?"

"Only the best mushrooms ever," Rowan enthused, brightening. "My father used to take me morel hunting when I was a kid. We would get enough to eat with our steaks for an entire weekend. Oh, they were so good. I haven't had them in years."

Ivy's expression was cocky as she smirked at Jack. "I told you they were good."

Quinn slid his eyes to Jack. "You don't think they're good?"

"Imagine eating a rubber bottle nipple, add a little grit, and then throw it up before eating it again. That's pretty much what morels taste like."

Rowan scowled. "You take that back."

"No." Jack shook his head. "I've been a good sport for two springs in a row. Last year I ate the morels because I was trying to get you to date me and I didn't want to offend you. This year I ate the morels because we were engaged and I thought maybe my taste buds were mistaken the previous year. They weren't wrong."

Quinn barked out a laugh as Rowan smiled. "Now I want to try these mushrooms, if only to say that I tasted them."

"You're better off not knowing," Jack countered. "I still have nightmares. Those mushrooms are worse than being shot."

Ivy's mouth dropped open. "Jack."

He offered her a lazy grin. "That was a bad joke." He decided to change the subject when she didn't immediately relax and return the smile. "So, I saw your security guys dealing with a situation on the tenth floor this morning. Did someone get drunk and fall off a balcony?"

"Someone got strangled," Rowan answered before Quinn could tackle the question in a more professional manner.

"Strangled?" Jack leaned forward, instantly alert. "Are you serious?"

Now that Rowan had opened the door, Quinn figured he had no choice but to walk through it. "Unfortunately, yes. We're not sure what happened. They specifically asked for the cameras to be shut off in that part of the ship so we're flying blind."

"Why would they ask for the cameras to be shut off?" Ivy asked.

"Because it's the bigwigs from that group I was telling you about," Rowan answered. "The ones that think movies, television, books, and music are rotting the brains of today's youth. They didn't want to be caught on camera — although I still think there's something weird about that — and now we don't know who went in or out of that room last night."

"That sucks." Jack was thoughtful. "It can't be easy to investigate a crime on a ship like this. What exactly are you allowed to do when it comes to making an arrest? Or even conducting an interrogation?"

"I have the power to take anyone and everyone into custody," Quinn replied. "You agree to that when you sign the paperwork for your rooms. I cannot technically arrest you, but I can put you in a holding cell. If you don't want to answer my questions, then I have the right to put you in a cell until we dock on the mainland."

"I guess I can see that." Jack was thoughtful. "You probably don't have a lot of murders on a cruise ship, though. If you need help with the investigation, I can offer any insight you might need. I'm a detective so I've investigated my fair share of murders."

Ivy scowled. "You've got to be kidding me," she muttered under her breath.

Quinn patted her arm by way of solace. "You don't have to worry about me taking him up on that. This isn't my first murder investigation either. I've got everything under control. There's nothing to worry about."

"Are you sure?" Jack pressed.

"I'm sure." Quinn was firm. The last thing he wanted was a Michigan cop infringing on his investigation. He might not have carried a badge, but he was good at his job and didn't need anyone muddying his waters. "You're on vacation. I thought the whole point of being on vacation was to spend time with the person you love."

"I thought that, too," Ivy grumbled.

Jack sighed as he reached across the table and snagged her hand. "I didn't mean to stick my nose into an investigation that's not mine. It was instinct. You're right, though. This is our vacation, honey. The only thing I want is to spend time with you."

Ivy could've been magnanimous, but that wasn't her way. "You have a funny way of showing it."

"How about we head back to the room, you change into your new bathing suit, and we head to that VIP pool we've heard so much about? I promise I'll show you exactly how much time I want to spend with you there."

Rowan beamed at Ivy as the woman relented. "That sounds like a good idea, huh? Maybe I'll stop by and see you guys later or something."

"Sure." Ivy bobbed her head. "We'll be around all day. It's not as if you can hide on a ship."

"Sometimes that doesn't feel true," Quinn said. "Hopefully we'll be able to put this issue to rest fairly quickly, though. I know I don't have to warn you because of your background, but keep your eyes open all the same.

"I have to believe Margaret Adkins was killed because of who she was, the agenda she was pushing," he continued. "There's still a killer out there. Make sure you're careful."

"Oh, I'm always careful where Ivy is concerned," Jack said as he stood. "Thanks for the warning, though. I'll keep her safe."

"You do that."

SEVEN

The swimsuit Ivy ultimately picked was plain. It was a simple blue color, solid straps and full coverage, and although it didn't have built-in foam cups or anything, Jack couldn't stop himself from calling it a "granny" swimsuit.

"I wish you would stop obsessing about the swimsuit," Ivy complained, a towel slung over her arm as she and Jack made their way to the VIP pool. "I think it's perfectly nice."

He slid her a sidelong look. "Honey, I don't care what you wear."

Ivy waited for him to continue. When he didn't immediately say anything else, she gave him a push. "But?"

"But nothing." Jack was firm. "I happen to like it when you wear those skirts that cover everything ... including your ankles. They give me ideas. The bathing suit is the same."

Ivy glanced down at the simple tank suit. "I just don't feel comfortable being on display. I'm never going to wear a bikini."

Jack's smile turned soft. "I don't care about that." He leaned closer to whisper so only she could hear him. "I think you forget that I get to see you naked whenever I want. Besides, you wear that coconut bra I like in the dreamscape."

Ivy hadn't really considered that and she tilted her head to the side as Jack held open a door for her. "Huh."

"That wasn't meant to be a suggestion that you take the coconut bra away from me in the dreams," Jack added hurriedly.

Not long after they met, something odd occurred. Ivy found herself drawn into Jack's dreams. That's how she knew the details of his shooting ... intimately. He relived the night his partner betrayed him and fired two bullets into his chest over and over again. And he suffered because of it.

Jack called Ivy into his dreams and she helped him work through it. She still wasn't sure why it happened. Jack was convinced she supplied the power and somehow recognized his need, but Ivy remained on the fence. That was hardly the only odd occurrence since they'd gotten together, though. Since then, Ivy had managed to see through the eyes of a killer, get a few psychic flashes, and even communicate with Jack on a very basic level when they were great distances apart.

She had no idea what to make of any of it.

"I'm not going to take your special treat away from you," Ivy said finally. "I simply never thought about it. I'm trying to figure out why I'm okay dressing in skimpy clothes in the dreamscape but not in real life."

It was early, so the VIP pool area was completely empty. Jack couldn't help being thrilled by the turn of events.

"I think I know why you're more comfortable in the dreamscape," Jack offered as he spread his towel out over a lounger.

Ivy looked to him expectantly.

"It's because you trust me."

She snorted. "Of course I trust you. I wouldn't marry someone I don't trust. Beyond that, though, I'm pretty sure I recognized that I could trust you the first day we met. We fought and kind of sniped at one another, but there was something about you that I couldn't stop thinking about."

"Yeah." Jack turned wistful. "I couldn't stop thinking about your skirts. I wondered if you wore underwear under them."

Ivy threw the bottle of sunscreen she carried at him, which he easily caught as he chuckled.

"You're so easy, honey," Jack teased.

"I'm not going to go there because it will lead to a fight," Ivy said after a beat. "We promised not to fight while we were on vacation."

"We promised to do our best not to fight," Jack clarified. "Fighting is what we do. Making up is what we do even better."

"Yes, well, I don't want to fight today." She stripped off her shorts and stared at the basic tank suit. "I do want you to finish what you were saying before, though."

"And what was that?"

"About me being more comfortable in the dreamscape."

"Oh, *that*." Jack's smile turned easy. "You're more comfortable in the dreamscape because it's just you and me. We don't judge each other. We accept each other for what we are, who we are. It's the same reason I'm more comfortable having my shirt off in the dreamscape than in public."

Ivy stilled. "You have an amazing body. It's so amazing I turn into one of those drooling women who lose the ability to think when you're without a shirt."

Jack's eyes warmed. "Thank you, honey. I feel the same way about you even though you insist on covering yourself like you're Amish sometimes. It's not that I think I'm fat."

"What is it?"

Jack sighed. "It's this." He pulled off his shirt, thankful they were the only ones at the pool, and tapped the scars close to his heart. "I don't like people looking at them because I can tell they're wondering what happened, what I did to deserve them."

Ivy's heart rolled. "Jack ... ."

"No, I know it's ridiculous. I don't like people staring at them. You don't like people staring at you because you think they're whispering behind your back. In truth, most people stare at you because you're beautiful ... and unique."

"Maisie and Ava?" Ivy let her dubious nature out to play, referring to two Shadow Lake women who made her temperature boil due to snide comments and rolled eyes.

"Those ladies are more hyenas than women," Jack countered, holding out the sunscreen so Ivy would have no choice but to cross to him to reclaim it. "You can't make everyone into a nice person. That's not how the world works. Most people, though, see perfection when they look at you."

"I think you're laying it on a little thick."

"I'm simply being truthful."

Ivy sighed as she held his gaze for a long beat. "You're really good for my ego."

"You're really good for my everything."

Ivy rested her fingertips on his scars as he drew her in for a hug. "You're perfect, Jack. Don't let anyone say anything different. Even when you're being a walking booger about the morels, you're still perfect."

"Oh. How can I not kiss you after that?" Jack didn't wait for an answer, instead pressing his lips to hers and offering a smoldering kiss that made Ivy's head spin. "I love you," he whispered against her ear. "For so many reasons."

"I love you, too." Ivy patted his back. "Now, you need to help me put this sunscreen on. I don't want to burn."

"Yes, ma'am."

"And after that, we'll vacation like nobody has ever vacationed before."

Jack snickered. "That sounds like a plan."

"WHAT AM I LOOKING AT again?"

Sally Jenkins, the head chef on The Bounding Storm, was supposed to be making a decision about changing her seafood distributor. Instead she was looking at a photograph featuring a woman with pink hair and her ridiculously attractive boyfriend while Rowan spouted nonsense that Sally couldn't quite follow.

"How many times do I have to tell you this?" Rowan's eyes flashed. "I need to know what this symbol means. You're the one who knew what the other symbols meant. How hard can it be to figure this one out?"

Sally wasn't used to Rowan being the one to fly off the handle. The auburn-haired photographer was the even-keeled one in their relationship. Sally was the one prone to fits of whimsy. "I'm not sure I even see a symbol," she said after a beat.

"You don't see a symbol?" Rowan was taken aback. "How can you not see it? Quinn sees it. I see it."

"Maybe I don't have your eagle eyes," Sally drawled, her annoyance coming out to play. "Maybe you should draw it for me or something."

"Fine." Rowan plucked the ink pen from Sally's hand and stole the notepad she was doodling on.

"Hey!" Sally made a face. "I'm doing actual work here."

"So am I." Rowan was firm. "I'm trying to figure out if this woman is in danger or if this symbol means something else entirely. You're our symbol expert."

"I grew up in New Orleans and recognize a few pagan symbols," Sally corrected. "I hardly think that means I'm a symbol expert."

"Yeah, well, you're better than me." Rowan finished her haphazard sketch and handed it to Sally. "It kind of looks like a woman, right?"

Sally furrowed her brow as she glanced between the sketch and the photograph. "Huh. Now that you mention it, I can see the symbol. That is so weird."

"Focus!" Rowan tapped the table for emphasis. "This could be important."

Sally had only been in on Rowan's big secret for a short amount of time, finding out by accident and then picking a fight until she could think things through. Ultimately, she realized it was Rowan's secret to tell – and she had plenty of reasons for wanting to keep it – and there was no reason to hold her self-preservation impulse against her. They'd been carefully feeling around each other ever since.

"It looks like the crone, Rowan," Sally said finally.

Rowan wasn't sure how to respond. "What do you mean? Crone?"

"It's a pagan symbol." Sally chose her words carefully. "There are several of them. The crone is one of them. It's a standard symbol, not good or bad. I'm not sure what it means in the grand scheme of things … especially from your perspective."

Whatever she was expecting, that wasn't it. Rowan sank into the chair across from Sally and stared hard at the drawing. "Give me your best guess," she said finally. "Why would this symbol show up in the same spot as the other symbols?"

"I don't know." Sally wished she had a way to help her friend. Rowan looked so morose she couldn't help but wonder if she'd disappointed the woman. "Maybe she's a priestess."

"I don't know what that means."

"A witch," Sally said finally, cringing when Rowan shot her an incredulous look. "Listen, I'm not the one who created the crone symbol, so you can wipe that look right off your face. I don't know what to tell you.

"The crone symbol is as old as the new world and it often referred to witches," she continued. "At home, in the French Quarter, a lot of tattoo artists use the crone symbol when creating one-of-a-kind works because people believe there's magic associated with it."

Rowan was perplexed as she rubbed her jaw. "Do you think witches are real?"

"Oh, definitely." Sally bobbed her head without hesitation. "I've seen some hinky stuff in my time. There are good witches and bad witches, by the way. White and dark, if you will. Not all witches are evil."

"Okay." Rowan sucked in a breath as she stared at the photograph. "So Ivy is a witch. Do you think she knows that?"

"Probably. Although ... how can you be sure that the symbol is referring to the woman?"

"Because it's a crone."

"Yeah, but that doesn't necessarily denote gender," Sally supplied. "Warlocks are witches, too. They're just witches with dingles and berries."

It took Rowan a moment to realize what Sally was saying. "That is ... so crass."

"You act as if you're surprised by that."

"I'm not but ... so crass."

Sally chuckled. "Yes, well, I'm a crass sort of person. As for this symbol, I don't know what to tell you. If Ivy Morgan is a witch, that doesn't necessarily mean she's in danger. Maybe your camera picked up on her magic and it was simply trying to alert you."

"Magic?" Rowan snorted. "You don't believe in magic, do you?"

"You see death omens in a camera," Sally reminded her. "I think the better question is, why don't you believe in magic? You're magic yourself."

"I hardly think ... ."

Sally wagged a finger to silence her friend. "And yet you are magic. Maybe you should try wrapping your head around that."

"THE WATER IS NICE."

Ivy stroked lazily next to Jack as they did laps. Swimming wasn't part of their normal routine. There was a river not far from Ivy's house — and a lake for that matter, too — but she preferred hiking to swimming. If she was going to get wet, she preferred it happening in the tub ... with bubbles.

Jack didn't immediately respond to the sound of Ivy's voice, his mind clearly somewhere else as they sliced through the water. She watched him for a bit as they made a turn to keep swimming, and then she shook her head.

"I've been thinking about running off with a biker gang," she offered. "I didn't think you would mind. It should only take six months or so to work my way through all of them. I'll see you when I get back."

Jack stirred. "I don't know. Where do you want to eat lunch?"

Ivy stopped swimming and planted her feet on the pool floor. "Where are you at?"

"What do you mean?" Jack shook himself out of his reverie and put his full focus on Ivy. "I'm swimming with you. Where else would I be?"

"You're not swimming with me. I just told you I was going to run off with a group of bikers for a sex party and you asked what I wanted for lunch."

Jack turned sheepish. "I didn't mean to get distracted."

Ivy waited.

"I was just thinking about the woman who died," he admitted. "Quinn said something that's been bothering me. He said the group asked for the cameras to be turned off in that part of a ship. I don't understand why he would acquiesce to that."

"Maybe there are certain privacy rules they have to follow."

"Yes, but people choose to take a cruise," Jack pointed out. "They don't own their rooms. They borrow them from the cruise liner. They shouldn't technically have rights like that."

"Maybe it's a respect thing."

"Maybe." Jack's gaze drifted again, causing Ivy to scowl.

"Hey!" She snapped her fingers in front of his face, causing him to jolt. "I thought we were supposed to be spending time together, vacationing like rock stars, drinking blue drinks by the pool, and all that other stuff."

Jack caught her hand before she could snap again. "I'm sorry, honey." His anger was more forceful than his regret when he started speaking, but the frustrated expression on her face shifted things quickly. "I really am sorry. It's just ... I find it weird that members of her own group were the ones to ask for the cameras to be turned off."

"And you think that suggests premeditation," Ivy finished. "I get it. That's the first thing that popped into my head, too."

"It is?" Jack couldn't contain his surprise. "Why didn't you say something?"

"Because I really don't care. I thought we were supposed to be relaxing."

Jack stared at her for a long beat. He spent two weeks worrying that everything would be perfect for their trip, no outside forces ruining anything, and now he was the one ruining things. "Honey, I'm sorry. I'll put it away." He dragged a hand through his damp hair. "Let's make some plans, huh? We can decide where we want to go for lunch and then maybe take a nap in one of those hammock things with the umbrellas we saw. How does that sound?"

Ivy merely stared at him. "Lunch sounds good," she said finally. "There's that salad bar place in the main promenade. You said we could try that."

"I am all for that." Jack was sincere. "Whatever you want."

"Well, I want a big salad."

"Great."

"I'm going to need a big meal if I plan on helping you question people about the dead woman."

Whatever he was expecting, that wasn't it. He practically tripped over his own feet as he moved to follow her toward the pool stairs. "What?"

"You heard me." Ivy wasn't in the mood for games. "You're not going to let this go. I'm not going to force you because it doesn't seem fair. You did all this for me. The least I can do is return the favor."

"No, no, no." Jack snagged her hand before she could exit the water, spinning her to face him. "You don't owe me anything. I wanted to do this for us. *Us*. Not just you."

"And yet you've gone out of your way to make this a big deal for me," Ivy pointed out. "If you want to spend a few hours asking questions about a dead woman because you're a workaholic, I don't want to stop you. I'll simply carry a blue drink with me as we wander around the ship."

"But ... ."

"No." Ivy shook her head, firm. "I'm serious about this. You can't stop thinking about it and I don't want to force you. I think we should work together — like we normally do — but make a plan to split time between work and fun."

"How do you mean?"

"We'll have lunch together. You'll spout more of those ridiculous lines about how you had no life before you met me and I'm the best thing that ever happened to you. Then we'll work for a few hours. Then we'll take a break for dinner so you can fawn all over me again. And then we'll go from there."

Jack grinned at her scheduling prowess. "How about I explain how you're the love of my life in between questioning people, too? How does that sound?"

Ivy shrugged. "I've had worse offers."

"Me, too." Jack stopped her from getting out of the pool by dragging her close, pressing her chest against his so he could stare into her eyes. "I really do love you. You have no idea how much."

"I think I know. I love you, too."

"Yeah, well, you're the best girlfriend ever."

Ivy smiled. "You can do better than that."

"You're not only the queen of my heart but the queen of all women."

"So schmaltzy, but I like where this is going."

"There's more. There's always more."

"Lay it on me."

8

EIGHT

Quinn tackled Joseph Guthrie right after breakfast. The man, who was in his late fifties, carried himself with an imperious air that grated the security chief the moment they exchanged pleasantries.

"I assume you're here about Margaret," Guthrie said as he sipped a club soda. "Another of our members, Richard Johnson, said you already questioned him. I couldn't believe it when word spread. Do you have a cause of death yet?"

"We do. She was murdered."

Guthrie's eyes widened. "I'm sorry but ... what?"

"She was strangled." Quinn opted not to go into specifics because he didn't want gossip flying fast and furious around the ship. Emily Little knew the basics of Margaret's death, but that didn't mean she would be able to fill in the finer details. "The doctor, who also serves as our medical examiner, is completing his report even as we speak."

"But ... I don't understand." Guthrie looked flummoxed. "I assumed she died of natural causes. That's what I heard."

"And who did you hear that from?"

"I'm ... not sure. Several people have been talking about it this morning."

"Yes, well, that's not the case." Quinn exuded authority as he flipped open his notebook. "We need to discuss a few things regarding your group."

"You can't possibly think someone in the group had anything to do with this."

"Murder is very rarely random," Quinn argued. "Those movies and television shows you see where serial killers lurk in every dark corner, they're not true. Murder is almost always done by someone the victim is familiar with. Since we're at sea, that means someone she knew killed her here ... and I would think that means it has to be someone from your group."

"But ... that's preposterous. The people in the National Organization for Clean Minds and Hearts are against the very thing you're talking about."

Quinn found it interesting that the man insisted on saying the organization's full name. "Yes, but it would seem to me that someone who didn't like what the group stood for, the message you were trying to spread, would actually infiltrate the group to get closer to Margaret," he pointed out.

"I didn't even consider that." Guthrie sipped his soda. "Okay, what do you want to know?"

"I need to know more about the formation of your group. I looked at your web page, but the specifics are very hazy. For example, how did you and Margaret meet?"

"Through church. We were part of Giving Souls Baptist Church."

"And that's in Folly Beach?"

"Yes."

"Did you know each other before the group started?"

"Um, yes and no. We were merely acquaintances when things started, but we were part of the same fellowship group. We got to talking about a murder case in that group one night, and things essentially spun from there."

"The Logan Luxemburg murder trial."

Guthrie bobbed his head. "Exactly. I see you've been doing your homework."

"That's my job." Quinn flipped to a new page in his tiny notebook.

"Once you started talking about that case, how quickly did you form the group?"

"Oh, not right away. It was more of a gradual thing. We talked in the fellowship group, everybody was outraged, and a few of us went out for coffee later that night and continued talking.

"The next week, the discussion returned to that subject but only for a brief period of time," he continued. "I was unhappy with that development — as were Brenda and Margaret — so we went out for coffee again. Those meetings became a weekly thing, to the point where we left the fellowship group, and slowly built our own group from there."

"That makes sense." Quinn jotted something down in his notebook. "The group started expanding at some point. How did that happen?"

"We made up fliers and handed them out at the church."

"And the church hierarchy was okay with that?"

"Absolutely. They thought our efforts were important, although I don't think anyone would've thought we'd make actual progress the way we have."

"And what progress is that?"

"We're meeting with our state representatives when we get back from the cruise. They're going to hear our petition and move forward from there."

"Have they said how they're going to move forward?"

Guthrie's face was blank. "I don't understand the question."

"Politicians meet with people all the time. That doesn't mean they're going to move on those platforms. In fact, most of the time, it's simply a placating measure so they can say they didn't ignore the issue."

"I don't think you understand how important our issue is." Guthrie turned haughty. "Video games are rotting the minds of the youth today."

"I can't argue with you there. I've never been a fan of video games."

Guthrie relaxed, although only marginally. "So you agree with our platform."

"Oh, not at all." Quinn shook his head. "I happen to love a good horror movie — mostly because my girlfriend does, but I find them entertaining, too — and I don't see the point of telling others what they can and can't watch. That's neither here nor there, though."

"It's the heart of the matter," Guthrie argued, annoyance flashing. "Violence on television begets violence in the real world."

"I don't happen to believe that's true. Movies don't make people violent. That's simply a convenient excuse because certain individuals don't want to curtail their poor impulses. Trust me. If there's a true psychopath out there, he or she is not going to be dissuaded because a horror movie or violent video game isn't available."

"You can't know that."

"And you can't know the opposite." Quinn wasn't in the mood to trade jabs regarding personal philosophies. "It ultimately doesn't matter, though, Mr. Guthrie. I need information about Margaret specifically. Did she have any enemies?"

"Of course she had enemies. We were trying to change the world. That always garners enemies."

"Okay, let me rephrase that. Did anyone lodge specific threats against her?"

"A lot of people did."

"I'm going to need a list."

"Fine. I'll see what I can put together. Solving Margaret's murder is important to me. She was a fine woman despite her difficulties. I want to help in your investigation, so give me a sheet of paper and I will write down some names."

"Great." Quinn ripped a sheet of paper from his notebook and handed it over. "While you're doing that, tell me exactly what difficulties you're talking about."

Guthrie grumbled something intelligible under his breath as he started writing.

"SHE WASN'T EASY TO GET along with."

Ivy and Jack found Brenda Farmer at the tiki bar after they finished lunch. They returned to their rooms long enough to change — Ivy refused to question people in a bathing suit — but started tracking down people of interest the moment they hit the deck. Their search quickly led them to Farmer, a forty-year-old woman with a blond helmet of hair and a desperate need to ramble.

"You've said that twice now," Jack noted as he leaned back in his chair, kicking his feet out in front of him. "Do you have any specific stories to go along with that observation?"

"I liked her, don't get me wrong," Farmer said hurriedly. She had a bubbly personality and an absolutely huge engagement ring glittering on her finger. The gold band that matched to signify the marriage was equally ornate. "We met through church."

"I believe I read that on the internet."

"Oh, are you interested in the cause?"

Jack wasn't sure how to answer, so he was happy when Ivy opted to do it for him.

"We heard several members of your group talking last night," Ivy supplied. "We were intrigued by the things they were saying, so we did some research. The growth of your group is impressive."

"That's because we have a very important message."

"It sounds like it." Ivy faked enthusiasm. "Margaret's death must have come as a shock to you given how much she was revered in certain circles."

"Oh, not that much of a surprise," Farmer said, sipping from a pink drink. Ivy had no idea what was in it, but she was intrigued enough to make a mental note for later. "Margaret was a passionate woman who believed in the cause with her whole heart."

"But?" Jack prodded.

"But she was also extremely difficult to deal with," Farmer replied. "She was ... very set in her ways. I guess that's the polite way to put it."

"What's the not-so-polite way?" Ivy asked.

"Well, she was a bully." Farmer offered up a rueful smile. "You probably think it's horrible for me to say that, but it's true. I'm not saying anything I didn't say to Margaret's face. She constantly went around telling people what they were doing wrong, how they had to fix things to make them right, and what she needed from them to be able to do her job."

"I'm not sure I follow," Jack said. "Why did she need things from others to do her job?"

"That's the exact same question I asked a hundred times and never got a firm answer. We weren't all that close. I mean ... we were close when we had to participate in joint interviews and everything, but the second the cameras were off we pretty much pretended the other didn't exist."

Ivy found the tidbit interesting. "Was it always that way between you?"

"Oh, no." Farmer shook her head, the hair refusing to lose its shape despite the breeze and movement. "When we were all in the fellowship group together, we were tight. It was only after that we stopped talking."

"There must have been an inciting event."

"I think it was more that a lot of little things built up rather than one big thing," Farmer volunteered. Ivy and Jack posed as an interested couple when they positioned themselves close to her and started asking questions. Thankfully, Farmer liked to talk and didn't find anything odd about the way they grilled her. "We were equals when we started, but by the time the group went national, suddenly Margaret was the star."

Understanding dawned on Ivy. "The attention got to her. That's what you're saying. She liked being in the limelight."

"She did," Farmer confirmed. "It was kind of frustrating because she would come to meetings and ask if we saw her on the news the night before. Since we weren't supposed to be watching television — we formed a boycott group — I didn't understand how she was seeing it."

Jack and Ivy exchanged a weighted look.

"Maybe someone told her about it," Jack suggested. "Maybe she didn't actually see it."

"Oh, I don't think that's true." Farmer pressed her lips together and gave the appearance of concentrating as she searched her memories. "She said how the camera added ten pounds so she was going on a diet and she needed to get better makeup because hers didn't look good on camera."

"Ah. I guess that means she did see herself on television."

"Yeah. People started talking about how she was kind of a hypocrite for watching television when the whole point of the group was to boycott stuff like that. She ignored the whispers, though. She only cared about the attention."

Curious despite herself, Ivy tapped her fingers on the table to draw Farmer's attention. "Who came up with the idea for everyone to go on a cruise together?"

"Margaret took credit for it, but Joe was the one who actually came up with the idea."

"Joseph Guthrie, right?" Jack asked. "He's one of the founders of your group, too."

"Yeah. It was originally him, Margaret, and me. Now I guess it's just me and him. We'll have to continue on with the group's legacy."

"And now you'll be the one on camera more often," Ivy pointed out. "I'm sure the news organizations will be waiting at port when we return to get interviews. This is bound to be a big story."

"Huh. I didn't consider that." Farmer brightened considerably. "I wonder if Joe and I should make plans on how we're going to split the attention. We don't want things to get out of control again right away."

"That's probably smart," Jack said. "Just one thing, though. I heard the security guards talking and they said something I found strange. I was hoping you would be able to explain it to me."

"Oh, yeah? What's that?"

"Someone in your group — the group of organizers, that is — requested for the cameras to be turned off in your block of rooms," Jack supplied. "Do you know who that was?"

"Oh, well ... ." Farmer knit her eyebrows. "I remember discussions about that, but I think Margaret made the ultimate decision."

That was not what Jack wanted to hear. "Okay, well, thanks for talking to us about your organization. You've given us a lot to think about."

QUINN TOOK A BREAK FROM relentless rounds of questions,

opting for an iced tea at the tiki bar as he claimed a reprieve from the sun.

"It is freaking hot out there," Quinn complained as he pressed the iced tea to his forehead. "Good grief. We should air condition the deck."

"That sounds like an easy task," Demarcus countered, grinning. "By the way, this is a cruise ship. If it wasn't hot on the deck, people wouldn't bother booking trips and we would be out of jobs."

"Good point." Quinn slammed half his iced tea and watched as an amused Demarcus topped it off. "I don't suppose you've heard any good gossip about Margaret Adkins, have you?"

"The dead chick? No. I've heard a lot of different stories about her death, though. Most people think she died of natural causes."

"Yeah. Every person I've questioned has said the same thing. I can't help but wonder if that's on purpose, like maybe members of the group are deliberately spreading that."

"That doesn't make a lot of sense to me. It seems that the violent death of their leader would be something to further propel the group. Why hide it when they can use it as a talking point on the evening news?"

Quinn hadn't even considered that. "Huh."

"Yeah."

"That is ... a very good point." Quinn was thoughtful as he swiveled on the stool and took a moment to look over the crowd at the bar. "This whole thing is odd to me. I didn't think much of it when the request to turn off the cameras came through. It's actually normal with some groups — especially corporate groups who don't want their game of multiple bedrooms recorded for posterity — but now that I think about this particular request, I'm a bit stumped."

"You think someone had this as a plan from the start, don't you?"

"I think that makes the most sense," Quinn confirmed. "She was strangled with a pair of nylons. That doesn't necessarily mean a woman did the deed, though. It probably took a decent amount of strength to hold Margaret down and tie the pantyhose around her neck.

"A woman could do that," he continued. "Rowan is certainly strong enough to pull that off if properly motivated. It would be easier for a man."

"Why would a man travel with pantyhose, though?" Demarcus asked.

"Because this was the plan all along. He might not have wanted to get caught with a weapon in his luggage. Weapons can make things messy, after all, and you don't want to risk walking through blood or firing a gun when someone could hear the noise and be drawn to the area and foul up an easy escape."

"I get what you're saying." Demarcus rolled his neck. "Your problem is that it's probably a member of the group ... and that's a lot of people to sift through."

"It is, but I can't help feeling that we're dealing with someone staying in that immediate bank of rooms. I'm going to have my men check the other video feeds to see if they can find a dude — or a woman, I wouldn't want to be sexist — walking around with pantyhose in his or her hands. I'm not holding out a lot of hope, though."

Demarcus barked out a laugh. "I can see that. I'm sure whoever did it shoved the nylons in a pocket."

"That makes the most sense. I still have to try. I ... ." Quinn trailed off when he saw a familiar figure chatting with Joseph Guthrie on the other side of the bar. "What's that about?"

Demarcus followed his gaze. "That's one of the heads of the group."

Quinn made a face. "I know that. I'm talking about the guy with him."

"The Bohemian princess's boyfriend. He's been talking to quite a few group members. I thought it was weird, too, but he's been asking a lot of questions."

Quinn was instantly suspicious. "What kind of questions?"

"The same questions I imagine you're asking. Did Margaret have any enemies? Was Margaret well liked? Can you think of anyone who would want to harm Margaret? By the way, I've heard a few of the answers. Margaret was definitely not liked."

"No, I got that impression, too," Quinn agreed, narrowing his eyes.

"I don't understand why Jack is asking questions of the guests, though."

"I thought he was a cop. That's what someone said."

"A *Michigan* cop. This isn't his jurisdiction."

"Okay. Calm down, tiger." Demarcus held up his hands in mock capitulation. "There's no reason to get all worked up."

"And there's no reason for him to be questioning the guests." Quinn drained his glass of iced tea and stood. "Seriously. It's like he's trying to irritate me."

"Or perhaps he's simply curious."

"No, he's trying to irritate me. I can feel it."

"Well, as long as you believe it, that's all that matters," Demarcus said. "If you're going over there to confront him, though, I would be careful. You're no longer the biggest dude on the boat. I think he might be able to take you."

Quinn snorted. "I'm still the king of the boat."

"If you say so."

NINE

Quinn plastered a tight smile on his face as he approached Jack. He expected the police officer to feign innocence, or maybe even slip out of the tiki bar before he could be questioned, but instead he merely quirked an eyebrow as the security chief slid into an open chair on the opposite side of the table.

"Hello, Quinn."

"Jack." Quinn took a seat at the table without being invited. "Where is Ivy?"

"She decided to take a break from the sun and head inside for a bit. We're not used to this extreme heat and she swears she's melting."

"She's fairly pale," Quinn agreed. "I'm guessing she doesn't get a lot of sun."

"She spends a decent amount of time outside. She's simply militant about sunscreen."

"That's smart. I should be better about it."

"Uh-huh." Jack sipped his drink, which looked to be simple tap water with a lime wedged on the rim for good measure. "And how are you doing today? Is your investigation proceeding well?"

"That's what I wanted to talk to you about."

"Really?"

"It seems I'm not the only one conducting an investigation."

Jack expected Quinn to figure out what he was doing at some point — although he was quicker than anticipated — so he saw no reason to lie. "I've been asking around," he confirmed. "I guess I can't turn off my inner cop. He's a persistent little bugger."

"You're on vacation."

"And I'm enjoying myself a great deal. Ivy has never been on a vacation — at least not one like this — and I'm determined to make sure she has a great time. If I'd known she'd never been on a vacation before, I would've tried to make this happen sooner."

The honesty caught Quinn off guard. "How long have you guys been together?"

"A little over a year. How about you and Rowan?"

"Not that long. She's only been on the ship a few months."

"Did you start dating right away?"

"Yes. Why do you care?"

"I'm simply curious."

Quinn exhaled slowly and ran his hand over the top of his short-cropped hair. "I pretty much fell for her the minute we met. I can't explain it. We started dating right away even though I wasn't in the market for a girlfriend and we haven't been apart since. I love her."

Jack's lips curved. "You sound like me. I moved to Shadow Lake because I needed a break from everything. I wasn't there two days when I met Ivy. She changed everything for me."

Even though he was irritated with Jack's insistence on poking his nose into a private investigation, Quinn found himself curious all the same. "You moved because you got shot. You didn't come right out and say that last night. You edged around it a little bit, but I could read between the lines."

"I was shot by my partner."

"Oh, man." Quinn cringed. "I didn't realize. I'm sorry. Did they catch him?"

"He died that night," Jack replied. "It was in a car chase. I was undergoing surgery at the hospital when it happened. I didn't know until I woke days later that he was gone."

"I've never been in your particular position, but I imagine that probably made things worse," Quinn noted. "I would've wanted to hunt him down myself and kill him."

"I didn't have that option, but upon waking in the hospital, I knew right away I needed a change. I had a lot of physical therapy to go through so I wasn't medically cleared to leave Detroit for almost six months. I was prepared for that moment and already had a new job lined up. I was eager to get out of the city."

"And move to the country. What's that like?"

"Different. It's ... quiet. There are little differences that you don't think about. Like street lamps. It's much darker in the country. When I sat in my yard in the city, I could see everything even after dark. When we sit in the backyard at home now, it's quiet except for the fire we build. It's dark enough to see the stars. I like it."

"The crime must be different, though. Don't you get bored?"

"No. You would actually be surprised how many big cases I've had since landing in Shadow Lake. It makes me appreciate the smaller ones. I like being able to come home at a decent hour most nights. I like that Ivy is usually there, cooking dinner, and ready to tell me about her day.

"Before, I worked twelve-hour shifts whether I was on the clock or not and had no one at home that I cared about," he continued. "I spent nights going to the bar with friends. There was no intimacy, though. No quiet nights watching movies or just talking."

Something about Jack's tone stirred Quinn. "I've never been a cop, but I understand what you're saying about the intimacy. Rowan and I don't technically live together, but we basically do. It's more difficult on a ship."

"I imagine. Will you guys stay here forever?"

"I doubt it. Rowan came here because she lost her job as a newspaper photographer. I came here after leaving the military because I didn't know what else I wanted to do and the money was good. I'm sure we'll figure out the rest moving forward."

Jack glommed on to part of Quinn's statement. "Newspaper photographer?"

"Yeah. Why?"

"It's just ... there was something familiar about her I couldn't place when we first met. I bet our paths crossed at crime scenes over the years."

"I hadn't even considered that," Quinn admitted. "You're probably right. In fact, I bet she heard about your shooting. One partner shooting another would've been big news."

"Yeah, well, I don't really like to dwell on that," Jack said. "That's part of my past, one that doesn't feel altogether real to me. Shadow Lake is my future. Ivy is my future. She's what matters most."

"That's nice."

"It is."

"If she's what matters most, though, why are you poking around my investigation? You should be enjoying your vacation."

"I can't help myself." Jack was rueful. "That camera thing bugs me. It makes me think that someone had this murder plotted out long before he or she arrived on the ship."

"I happen to believe that, too. It's still not your investigation."

"No," Jack agreed. "Ivy has given me permission to ask a few questions, though. She helped me for a bit before lunch. She lost interest quickly, though. She's just happy to be away from work. I have no intention of ruining things for her."

"You're not going to stop asking questions, though, are you?"

"No."

"Why do you have to be such a pain?"

Jack chuckled. "You sound like Ivy."

"I'm starting to like her more and more with each passing moment."

"That's something she would say."

"You're really starting to irritate me."

IVY WASN'T A SUN WORSHIPPER so the heat beat her down quickly. As much as she wanted to spend time with Jack, she needed a break so she headed inside. She perused the stores, purchased an iced tea from the coffee shop, and then simply walked the hallways. She lost interest in that after about an hour and was relieved to find Rowan sitting in a small parlor working on her computer. At least she had someone to talk to now.

"Hey."

Rowan glanced up from her screen and smiled. "Hey. What are you doing inside? It's a beautiful day."

"It is, but I'm not used to this heat," Ivy admitted. "It's sucking the life right out of me. I don't know how to explain it. All I want to do is take a nap, but it's like sleeping in a furnace on the deck."

Rowan chuckled. "You sound like me when I first got here. I thought I would never survive. I sweated so much I lost five pounds just in water weight the first week. I eventually adjusted."

"I'm not going to be here long enough to adjust. That means frequent breaks for me."

"That doesn't sound so bad." Rowan lifted her chin so she could study the direction Ivy came from. "Where is Jack?"

"He's on deck questioning people about the murder." Ivy blurted it out without giving it much thought. "He can't help himself. It's a mystery and he wants to solve it. I don't know why he can't leave the cop at home, but it's seemingly impossible."

"Quinn isn't going to like it if he catches Jack asking the guests questions."

"I figure that's their problem. Besides, they're already sizing each other up. I don't know if you've noticed, but they seem a bit ... quietly competitive, I guess would be the correct term ... when they're around each other."

Surprised, Rowan leaned forward. "I thought I was the only one who noticed that. Quinn keeps puffing his chest out like he's absorbing testosterone from the sun or something."

Ivy giggled. "It's got to be a man thing. My brother Max would probably be doing it, too. When Jack and I first started dating, I swear there were times when I caught Max and Jack comparing muscles when they thought no one was looking."

"Oh, that is hilarious. Did you say something?"

"Of course. They both denied it. Once, though, Max caught Jack in my driveway — there was a dead body there days before; it's a long story — and he tried to wrestle him down. Jack was stronger, though, and he wrestled Max down. My brother still hasn't gotten over it."

"Well, Jack is trained, too."

"That's Max's excuse." Ivy flicked her eyes to Rowan's computer screen. "Are you working? I can leave you alone so you can focus."

"Oh, you don't have to worry about that," Rowan said. "I'm loading photos to the portals. I have to do that at least three times a day. I usually do it in the tiki bar, but it's so hot today I decided to take advantage of the air conditioning. You're not bothering me. It simply takes a bit of time for the photographs to load."

"Do you have a minimum of photos you're supposed to take a day?"

"No. I'm supposed to get as many people as possible, though."

"Did you always want to be a ship photographer?" Ivy was honestly curious. "Do they have a course on that or something?"

"I never saw this in my future," Rowan replied. "Trust me. This was so far from my mind I'm not sure it even existed in the dark corners. I went to school for photography with a focus on photojournalism. Unfortunately, the state of journalism today is such that I lost my job and had to come up with a new plan."

"You were a newspaper photographer?"

Rowan bobbed her head. "I was. I liked my job. I was good at it. It went away overnight, though, and I had to come up with a different plan."

"I wonder if you met Jack while out on the job."

"What?"

"Jack was a Detroit police officer. You were a photographer in the area. It would only make sense to meet under different circumstances. Jack thought you looked familiar, but he couldn't place you."

"It's weird, but I thought both of you looked familiar."

"Yeah. You would know Jack's story, though." Ivy rubbed her palms against her knees. "He was the police officer shot by his partner. I don't know if you remember that."

Rowan's mouth dropped open. "I remember. It was a huge deal. There was a manhunt for the partner. I was out with a reporter because people were trying to track him down. He died in an accident or something."

"That's it." Ivy bobbed her head. "Jack almost died. It took six months of physical therapy for him to get back on his feet. He moved to Shadow Lake not long after."

"That was a huge story. I'm sorry that happened to him."

"I am, too, although ... ." She left it hanging.

"Although if he hadn't gotten shot he never would've moved to Shadow Lake and you two wouldn't have found each other," Rowan finished. "It's okay. I know how that is. I thought losing my job was a terrible thing until I met Quinn. We wouldn't have found each other otherwise, so I get it."

"It's terrible to admit, but I wouldn't change anything. I like how things turned out."

"I don't think you have to worry about that," Rowan teased. "Jack seems to like how things turned out, too."

"Yeah. He's still a cop at heart, though, which is why he's questioning people on our vacation."

"You don't seem that worked up about it."

"No, I ... hey, what's that?"

It took Rowan a moment to realize Ivy was staring at her computer screen. "What's what?"

"That thing on that photo of Margaret Adkins."

Rowan's heart did a long, slow somersault. "What thing?"

"There's a symbol or something in the corner of the photo." Ivy squinted in an attempt to see better. "What is that?"

"I don't know." Rowan chose her words carefully. "It's probably just a shadow. I've been wondering if there's something wrong with my camera, though, because I saw a different type of shadow in one of your photos. Let me show you."

Rowan closed out of the portal window and clicked on a desktop folder. The photographs of Ivy were on top, and she clicked on one before turning the laptop so Ivy could better see the image. "Do you see a symbol here, too?"

"I do," Ivy answered right away. "It's right there." She pointed at the corner of the photo. "I know this sounds strange, but it looks like an old woman."

"That's what I said," Rowan agreed. "I showed the photo to my friend and she didn't see the shadow. It's odd. I'm trying to figure out if it's a shutter glitch, or maybe something with the aperture."

"I don't know a lot about cameras," Ivy admitted. "It's weird, though. I don't know what to make of it."

Rowan felt bad lying, but she was militant about keeping her ability a secret. The only people on the ship who knew were Quinn, because she told him when she needed help saving a life, and Sally, because she accidentally found out. Both were trustworthy. And, while Rowan believed Ivy was trustworthy, too, she didn't know her well enough to take the risk.

"I might re-set the camera to factory settings and see if that corrects it," Rowan lied. "The camera is new. Quinn bought it for me as a gift a few weeks ago. I was having a hard time and he wanted to make me feel better. He took me on a mini-vacation, although we just checked into a hotel for a few days because we couldn't spare an entire week."

"That sounds nice, though." Ivy turned away from the photo and focused on Rowan. "You guys seem happy together. Quinn's need to thump his chest when Jack is around notwithstanding, he seems like a nice guy."

"He is. He's the best guy. Although, I think Quinn's biggest problem is that Jack is taller than him. Quinn likes to be the big man on the ship."

Ivy choked on a laugh. "That seriously sounds like Max. Max was like the tallest guy in Shadow Lake before Jack joined the police department. He's still not over Jack usurping his throne."

"It probably helps that he's not in competition with Jack for female attention."

"I think that's the only reason they haven't killed each other," Ivy agreed.

"Not the only reason. They both love you. That will hold them together forever, too."

Ivy smiled. "Probably. Tell me about living on a cruise ship. I'm dying to hear what that's like. I bet it's fun."

"There's never a dull moment. That's the one thing I can say with absolute certainty. Come on, though. I'll show you my room — which is vastly different from your room — and we'll see if you think the notion of living on a ship is so romantic after that."

TEN

"This isn't going to turn into a playground wrestling match, is it?"

Ivy, in the bathroom changing her clothes for dinner, had listened to Jack relate how he spent his afternoon for a full twenty minutes before making her true feelings known.

Jack scowled as he smoothed his shirt. "No. Quinn and I actually had a nice conversation, if you must know."

Ivy wasn't sure she believed him. "I've seen you two together. You're one step away from thumping your chests and baying at the moon."

"Oh, what a pretty picture, honey. I ... ." Jack forgot whatever he was going to say when Ivy appeared in the bathroom doorway. The fact that she was wearing a dress even though she preferred skirts wasn't necessarily a surprise. She wore the occasional dress, although the situation had to specifically call for it. This dress, though, was something else entirely.

It was simple — Ivy would never do fancy — but it was short enough that it fell just above her knees. It was blue tie-dye with spaghetti straps that showed off her shoulders. And even though Ivy's skin remained pale, she practically glowed under the soft gel lights of the bathroom.

"Oh, wow." Jack exhaled slowly as he drank in her appearance. "You look amazing, honey."

Ivy cocked an eyebrow. "That's quite the reaction for a simple dress. I bought it in one of the gift shops this afternoon." She furrowed her brow as she glanced at her reflection in the full-length mirror. "You don't think it's too ... casual ... do you?"

Jack snickered. "No. I think you look amazing."

"Are you sure?"

Ivy never suffered from bouts of insecurity so Jack knew better than to tease her.

"I think you're the most beautiful woman in the world," he answered honestly. "I think every other woman pales in comparison to you. I thank my lucky stars every day that you're mine."

Instead of melting, Ivy made an exaggerated expression. "That was ... I don't even know what to say."

"Romantic?"

"Ridiculous."

Jack snickered and held out his hand. "That doesn't mean it's not true. You're beautiful, honey. I am curious what possessed you to buy a new dress, though. You're pretty particular about your clothes."

Ivy shrugged. "I don't know. I needed time out of the sun and was wandering around the stores because there wasn't much else to do without you and I saw it. If you don't like it, I can change."

"No, no, no." Jack grabbed her hand and dragged her to him. "I love it ... and you. I'm also sorry about this afternoon. I shouldn't have abandoned you to question people about a murder that's not even in my jurisdiction."

Ivy stared at him for a long beat. "It wasn't my favorite part of the day, but it was hardly the end of the world. I ran into Rowan and we talked about stuff. I like her."

"Wow. That's two women you've managed to make friends with in the space of a few months," Jack teased. "First Harper and now Rowan. If I didn't know better, I would think you were softening."

"Don't push things." Ivy extended a warning finger. "Most women don't like me. I can't explain it."

"You're different and people are jerks."

"I don't have that problem with men."

"That's because you're beautiful and men like women who are different. How else do you explain the fact that I fell head over heels for you the second I saw you?"

"I don't think it was the first second."

"I think it was pretty close."

Ivy impulsively leaned closer and pressed her head to Jack's chest for a moment. "It's okay that you wanted to ask questions about Margaret Adkins. I get it. You can't turn off what you are and I don't want you to change. I like you the way you are."

"You wish I would've spent that time with you, though."

"No. I'm a big girl. I can take care of myself."

Jack stroked the back of her head. "This is a special occasion for both of us. I shouldn't have left you on your own. If you want to know the truth, I think part of it was the fact that I like messing with Quinn. He's kind of funny."

Ivy chuckled. "I figured that out myself. You have a special ability to needle people that I truly admire."

"It won't happen again." Jack cupped her chin and stared into her eyes. "I'm sorry. I want to be with you. That's why I booked this trip in the first place. It won't happen again. I promise."

Ivy didn't go gooey and throw her arms around him. Instead, she snorted. "Oh, it's going to happen again. You won't be able to help yourself."

"I'm in control of my actions."

"I bet you a really long massage that you're back to asking questions by lunch tomorrow."

"You're on."

"I DON'T UNDERSTAND WHY you're so worked up about this," Quinn said as he watched Rowan saunter out of the bathroom. She was dressed in a pretty yellow slip dress, the color making her features look somehow brighter, and he liked the way the flip skirt danced around her legs. "I've seen the symbol before. Obviously you're not the only one who can see it."

"You saw it after I pointed it out to you," Rowan explained, grabbing her purse from the dresser and looking inside to make sure her keycard was accounted for. "I remember that day very well. I was upset because I saw the omen in a photograph. I didn't know what to do. I needed your help. I showed you the omen in the photo, convinced you wouldn't be able to see it, but you surprised me and not only saw the omen but believed what I was telling you. You didn't see it before I showed you the photo."

"I'm not sure that's exactly fair," Quinn argued. "I wasn't spending all my time following you around and looking at photos over your shoulder. I might have seen the omen on my own. We'll never know. Now I know what to look for."

"Yeah, but ... Ivy saw it clear as day."

"I don't know why that's important."

"It's important because no one led her to answers. She found questions on her own."

"Wow, that was almost poetic, sweetheart," Quinn teased, poking her side to cajole a smile. "Do you want to know what I think?"

"Probably not."

Quinn barreled forward anyway. "I think you like Ivy and want to ascribe motivations and potential that probably don't exist."

"I do like her but that doesn't change the fact that she recognized the symbol. She recognized multiple symbols. I showed her a variety of photos and she saw the symbols in all of them. I even dug out old photos to be sure."

Quinn heaved out a sigh. She obviously wasn't going to let this go. "Okay, she can see the symbols." He searched for an explanation. The one he came up with was interesting. "Do you think it's possible that she's like you?"

"She doesn't even take photos. She said she doesn't know anything about cameras."

"See, I'm not sure this ability of yours — whatever it is — has anything to do with you being a photographer," Quinn hedged. "I've often wondered if you're capable of doing other things. Given everything that's going on with your father, though, I didn't want to bring that up until things were more settled."

"I don't even know what to say to that. What does that mean?"

"I think maybe you're capable of other things."

"Like what?"

"I have no idea, but if Ivy is capable of other things, she might actually be able to lead us to answers," Quinn replied. "I did some research on what you told me. The symbol that looked like a little woman. Sally called it the crone, right?"

Rowan nodded.

"The crone basically referred to a witch in olden times," Quinn explained. "I think that was probably an easy way to refer to someone with magical abilities, but who knows? Ivy has a penchant for dressing a certain way and carrying herself with authority. Maybe she is a witch."

"I don't think witches are real," Rowan argued.

"And I didn't think photographers seeing omens in pictures was a thing until I met you," Quinn supplied. "I was thrown for a loop at the start of it, but the more I think about it, the more I'm starting to wonder if there's more than one type of magical being out there."

Rowan tilted her head to the side, considering. "I'm not sure I like being referred to as 'magical.' It's kind of weird ... and hokey."

"Well, you're going to need to get used to it. You are magical. The things you can do are magical. I find everything about you magical. You need to suck it up."

Rowan turned rueful. "I think you're just saying that to soften me up so I throw myself at you and rain kisses all over your face."

Quinn's grin was mischievous as he wrapped his arm around her waist and tugged her body so it was flush with his. "I like the idea of you raining kisses on me."

"Oh, yeah?"

He nodded as he lowered his mouth to hers. The kiss was simple, sweet. It also promised more for later. "That's better," he sighed as he rested his cheek against her forehead. "Have I mentioned how much I love you?"

"I love you, too. That doesn't change the fact that I think there's something different about Ivy."

"That doesn't mean it's something bad."

"Oh, I don't think it's bad." Rowan's lips curved against his shoulder. "I think it's going to be interesting, though."

"Then I'm looking forward to figuring out exactly what secret she's hiding with you."

"I guess we have a plan, huh?"

"We definitely do."

"I'M AMAZED AT THE VEGETARIAN offerings this ship has," Ivy said as she settled at a small table with Jack in the dining room. She was careful as she arranged the skirt of her dress to make sure it didn't accidentally fly up, something Jack found amusing. "They have at least three choices at every meal. Most places would offer a salad and be done with it."

"That was one of the questions I asked when I called," Jack admitted. "I was worried because cruise ships are known for seafood and fried American fare. If you couldn't eat, I was going to pick a different vacation."

"Oh, yeah?" Ivy was officially intrigued. "Like what?"

Jack shrugged. "I don't know. We haven't really talked about our honeymoon yet. Where do you want to go?"

The question caught Ivy off guard. "I haven't really thought about it either," she admitted. "I've been so busy arguing with my mother about the fact that I want a small wedding and I'm not sure about wearing white that I haven't had a lot of time to think about other things."

"You're not wearing white?"

Ivy shrugged. "I haven't decided yet. I might go with some color ... unless you don't like that idea. Do you want a traditional wedding?"

"I just want you. I don't care about the type of wedding we have. If you want to strip down naked and get married in the backyard, I'm totally up for that."

Ivy didn't want to encourage him, but she couldn't stop herself from laughing. "I don't think that will be necessary."

"Yes, well, I'm open to suggestions." Jack cracked a crab leg and dipped it in butter. "Is there a specific reason you don't want to wear white?"

"I don't know. I'm not a virgin so ... white is for virgins."

"I think that's an oversimplification," he countered. "That's what it was supposed to mean a long time ago. Now it's simply tradition."

"Yeah." Ivy scrubbed her cheek. "I was thinking about more of a rose white, but if you want a traditional white dress, I'm sure I can figure something out."

Jack held up his hand to still her. "Wait ... what color is rose white?"

"It's white with a hint of pink."

"So you are wearing white."

"Rose white. It's not the same as traditional white."

"Women," Jack muttered, shaking his head. "I have news for you, honey, all those colors you don't think are white because they're a tiny bit different, well, men think of all fifty thousand of those colors as white. I should've realized what you were talking about after we painted the basement together and you tried to tell me cream and ecru were different colors."

"They are."

"Only to a woman." He snickered at her indignant expression. "It doesn't matter. I was simply surprised when you said you weren't wearing white. Now that I know you really are wearing white, we can put that behind us and focus on other things."

"Like what?"

"Like what kind of cake do you want? I'm leaning toward chocolate even though it might not be traditional."

"Nice save."

"I thought so." Jack winked as she shoveled lasagna into her mouth. "If you don't want to talk about cake, we can talk about something else. I'm still keen to talk about our honeymoon. Where do you want to go?"

Since honeymoon talk was happier than arguing about different shades of white, Ivy shifted her attention. "There's a beautiful campground in the Upper Peninsula, a place that has like fifty small water-falls to hike to. We could go there."

Jack made a face. "Do you remember the last time we went camping?"

"Yes."

"Do you think you'll ever get me to go camping again after that trip?"

Ivy chuckled. "Actually, I'm willing to bet you give in and go camping with me again if I press you on the issue. You're too giving to take camping away from me. It's probably not a honeymoon thing, though. I ... ." She didn't get a chance to finish because at that exact moment, the hair on the back of her neck stood on end as a loud crash filled the air. In the split second after, the room was plunged into darkness.

"Jack?"

"I'm here, honey." Jack shifted so he could see the wall closest to them, sighing in relief when the emergency lights kicked on. They weren't overly bright but would allow them to escape from the dining room. "I think the power simply flashed because it's storming out."

As if on cue, another rumble of thunder filled the air.

"It's just a storm," Ivy murmured, although the idea didn't sit well with her. "How are we supposed to get back in our rooms if the keycards don't work?"

"I'm not sure," Jack replied honestly. "I think we should get out of here until the lights come back on, though. I don't like sitting here mostly in the dark like this. It makes me feel claustrophobic."

"Okay." Ivy instinctively reached over the table and found Jack's hand waiting for her. "How did you know I was trying to touch you?"

"Because I always want to touch you. Come on."

The trip to the exit door wasn't exactly easy. Jack and Ivy weren't the only ones to embrace the idea of escape. The bulk of the people eating opted to stay in their seats — which was probably wise — but Jack wasn't a fan of feeling closed in. Ever since he was shot in the chest and left to die in an alley, his lung not properly inflating and causing him to feel as if he was being smothered, he hadn't been a fan of oppressive darkness and closed spaces. Technically the dining room was open and airy, but the lack of light made Jack feel otherwise.

"We'll find a spot away from everyone," Jack suggested, keeping a firm grip on Ivy as they weaved through the confused people. "We'll just take a break."

Ivy didn't like the stress she heard in his voice, but she wisely opted against commenting on it. "That sounds good."

"Stay close, honey. This place is a madhouse."

"I'm with you ... always."

Jack squeezed her hand. "That's just the way I like it."

Ivy remained focused on what was ahead of her and tuned out everything else, until it was almost like being trapped in an echo chamber. Technically people were talking and conversing — and panicking — on every side of her, but she focused on nothing but Jack. They were close to the exit doors, she knew that, but they still had several small groups to fight their way through.

It was in the middle of one of these groups when Ivy's muffled world fell away and something else came into sharp focus. For one brief moment, Ivy wondered if she'd been called into a dream. That was the only thing she could think of to explain what she was seeing ... and feeling. That didn't fit the scenario, though. Her hand was still clasped tightly with Jack's and she was aware they were in the dining room. The other vision, though, was loud, brash, and overbearing.

Ivy stumbled as she tried to absorb what she was seeing, quick flashes of screaming and violence momentarily overwhelming her. She lost her footing as she tried to keep up, images of another place cascading through her mind at a fantastic clip.

Ivy recognized she was falling but couldn't force her body to react quickly enough to remedy the situation. All she knew was that the floor was racing up — or perhaps she was racing down, she wasn't sure — and an impact was imminent.

Instead, at the very last second, Jack swooped in and caught her, using his powerful muscles to suspend her momentum and press her to his chest.

"Ivy, are you okay?"

Ivy gasped in response.

"Honey?" Jack's eyes filled with worry as she forced herself to focus on his handsome face. "Are you okay? Did something happen?"

"I don't know." Ivy had no idea how to explain what she saw. The images were a mess in her head. "Get me out of here, Jack. There are too many people. I can't breathe."

"I've got you." Jack hoisted Ivy to her feet and pulled her in front of him, using his body as a shield at her back as he carefully cleared a path toward the door. "We're almost there. I'll have you outside in a second."

"Great. I'll be able to breathe then."

"Me, too." He tightened his grip on her out of instinct. "And then you can tell me what just happened, because I'm dying to know."

"I'm not sure you're going to feel that way after."

"Well, we'll figure it out either way. You're stuck with me for life, for better or for worse. You'll tell me and we'll figure out what's to be done."

"I'm not sure anything can be done."

"We won't know until we talk about it. Come on."

ELEVEN

The power outage was brief.

By the time Jack got Ivy to an open spot in the corner of the lobby, the lights were back on and the rest of the guests seemed happy to forget about the short interruption and return to whatever they were doing beforehand.

Jack wasn't that easily settled.

"What happened?" He pushed Ivy's hair away from her face and stared into her sea-blue eyes.

"I saw something." Ivy wasn't sure how to explain what happened during the melee. "It was almost more like I felt something ... from inside someone else's head."

Most other men would've balked at the explanation. This was hardly the first time Ivy had done something fantastical, though. "Tell me."

"It was weird."

"I'm used to weird. I like weird."

Ivy managed a ghost of a smile. "You would have to like weird to be with me, huh?"

"In your case I love weird. I was talking about your brother when I said I liked it."

That got a full-blown laugh from Ivy, although it was only a short burst and then she sobered. "I was trying to tune everyone else out. I don't like crowds. I focused on your hand ... and putting one foot in front of the other. I just wanted to get out."

"You and me both. I don't like feeling penned in."

"No. I know." She patted the spot above his heart, where his scars were located, and swallowed hard. "I think I went into some form of a trance. I don't know how else to explain it. I saw the view off the deck of the ship ... and someone was screaming ... and I could smell blood. It has a distinctive smell."

"I know, honey." He kissed her cheek. "Did you see what the woman looked like?"

Ivy shook her head. "No. It was more like I was seeing things from her point of view, if that makes sense."

None of it made sense to Jack. This wasn't the first time she'd witnessed something through someone else's eyes, though. "You've done this before."

"I've found myself in the head of a killer," Ivy countered. "This time I was in the head of the victim. I didn't think anything could be worse than feeling what a predator feels. I was wrong. I don't like being the prey."

Jack was uncomfortable with the way she phrased it. "I won't let anything happen to you. I mean it."

Ivy nodded. "I know." She rubbed her forehead. "I want to go to bed. I know it's early but ... I don't want to be out here any longer. We can't enjoy the deck anyway. It's storming."

"You didn't get to eat anything."

"I'm not hungry."

Jack had no intention of letting that stand, but pushing her now would only make matters worse. "Come on." He linked his fingers with hers and directed her toward the elevator. "We'll go back to the room, get comfortable, and order room service. We'll lock ourselves away from everyone for the rest of the night."

"You don't have to do that. I can go back to the room by myself."

"Absolutely not." Jack was firm as he pressed the button to the elevator. "You're stuck with me for the rest of the night."

Ivy laid her head on his shoulder. "The rest of my life."

"Definitely. It's you and me forever. Besides, I like the idea of it just being the two of us for the rest of the night. There's no one else I would rather spend my time with."

"Me, too."

"WHY DID THE POWER go out?"

Quinn met the ship's captain Michael Griffin in the control booth, his confusion on full display. Rowan was with him, her nerves frayed, but Michael barely glanced at her in the face of Quinn's pointed question.

"It was a storm surge," Michael replied calmly. "It's not a normal thing, but it occasionally happens. Lightning hit the water close to us, caused a temporary disruption, but we rebooted the system and it's fine. We have backups upon backups for situations like this."

Quinn was momentarily placated. "Oh."

"So it wasn't something a guest did or anything?" Rowan queried. "You're sure of that, right?"

"I'm definitely sure of that," Michael confirmed. "We've been through this before. It's not common, but it has been known to happen. Everything is back up and running, though."

Quinn relaxed his stance, the worry that had been coursing through him dissipating. "Well, if you say it's normal, I guess I have to believe you."

"It's not normal, but this is hardly the first time it's happened. I've been through it three times over the course of my career. That storm came out of nowhere — which happens on the open seas — and it's going to last at least another hour or two. We should be fine, though. We're lowering our speed, just to be on the safe side, but we'll be through to the other side by ten."

"That's a relief." Quinn flicked his eyes to Rowan and offered her a rueful smile. "I guess I freaked out for nothing, huh?"

"We both freaked out for nothing," Rowan corrected. "I thought it had to be something else. I didn't realize lightning was an issue on the water. Now that I think about it, though, I feel kind of stupid for not realizing it."

"We plan on sending out complimentary dessert baskets to all the rooms to keep the guests happy," Michael said. "I've already ordered for it to happen. The guests will return to their rooms, eat some cookies, and then probably have sex because cookies make most people want to have sex."

Quinn made an exaggerated face. "What world are you living in that cookies make people want to have sex? That's not a thing." He looked to Rowan for confirmation. "Right?"

Rowan shrugged, noncommittal. "I could eat a cookie."

He snickered despite himself. "I'll give you a cookie." He poked her side before shaking his head and turning back to Michael. "Is there something I should be doing to reassure the passengers?"

"I'm getting reports from all around the ship. Everything seems to be back to normal. Go back to what you were doing and have a nice night. Not everything is cause for panic."

"I'll try to keep that in mind."

"You do that."

ROWAN WASN'T QUITE READY to let go of her anxiety once she and Quinn hit the tiki bar. Thankfully, because of the storm, the bulk of the guests opted to remain indoors. That gave them the run of the place — other than Demarcus — to talk over a few things.

"I thought for sure someone killed the lights so they could commit another murder," she admitted as Demarcus delivered a rum runner to her before she could place an order. "What is this?"

"You look like you need alcohol to settle," Demarcus replied, handing Quinn a Corona before plopping in a chair. "I need to get off my feet so I was simply trying to get ahead of your orders."

"That's very nice of you," Rowan said dryly, making a face as she sipped her cocktail. "This is strong."

"You look like you have a lot of settling to do."

Quinn chuckled, genuinely amused. "He's not wrong. That will probably take the edge off for you, which I'm not opposed to."

Rowan muttered something under her breath that Quinn couldn't quite make out. It sounded like "I'll show you my edge," but he couldn't be sure. Either way, he was keen to avoid an argument so he opted to pretend he didn't hear the disagreeable words. "Did you lose power up here, Demarcus?"

"I did." The weary-looking bartender nodded. "It was freaky. I was up here alone and the power died at the exact second a huge bolt of lightning hit the water. It felt close — like ridiculously close — and I could actually feel my hair standing on end."

"That is freaky," Rowan said, clucking her sympathy. "What did you do?"

"I had a drink to calm myself."

"No wonder you're so chill," Quinn teased. "Although ... are you supposed to be drinking on the job?"

"Bite me. It was dark as a crypt up here. You have no idea. Without the lights on the walkways around the deck, it was eerie. Like ... ghost movie eerie."

"Well, I guess I'll let it go this one time," Quinn said. "I probably would've started drinking under those circumstances, too."

"I definitely would have," Rowan agreed, taking another sip of her rum runner. "This is good."

"You haven't eaten dinner yet," Quinn reminded her. "You might want to take it slow so you don't tip into drunk territory without realizing it."

"Yes, sir." Rowan mock saluted as her eyes fired. "Whatever you say, sir."

"Oh, geez." Quinn rolled his eyes. "Why are you purposely trying to make my life difficult?"

"I think that's your imagination, sir," Rowan shot back. "I'm being a diligent employee, sir."

Demarcus's amusement was obvious as he attempted to hold back a chuckle ... and failed. "I would definitely get some food into her."

"That's the plan," Quinn acknowledged. "We simply wanted to check in with you before heading inside. You haven't heard or seen anything else of interest tonight, have you?"

"Um ... I saw the personal assistant of the dead woman tying one on in the Neptune Bar & Grill a few hours ago. She looked to be drowning her sorrows with an audience."

"What audience?" Rowan asked, abandoning her efforts to irritate Quinn. "Who was she with?"

"Other members of that group, including the two who will share duties as the face of the organization now that Margaret Adkins is dead."

"Joseph Guthrie and Brenda Farmer?" Quinn queried.

"Yup. They were both there partying, too."

"That's interesting. Did anyone seem to be mourning Margaret's death? From what I understand, she wasn't exactly well-liked. Still, you would think they'd at least pretend to be sad over her passing."

"You would think," Demarcus agreed. "No one in that group looked sad. Of course, once you're drunk, normal emotions sometimes go out the window. They might wake up regretting their actions tomorrow morning."

"Somehow I doubt that." Quinn slid his gaze to Rowan and found her watching him with contemplative eyes. "I don't see where there's anything we can do about their carousing tonight. I'll question them tomorrow to see if I can get more out of them. Right now, we're at something of a standstill. A lot of people hated Margaret. Only one of them killed her, though, and it isn't easy to narrow down the suspect pool."

"I think they'll all have hangovers tomorrow, so maybe they will let something slip if you go at them hard enough," Demarcus suggested. "The only other thing I saw was your Bohemian princess right after the power was restored. She looked a mess."

"What do you mean by that?" Rowan asked, instantly alert.

"Just that she was white as a ghost and seemed upset," Demarcus replied. "I went to check the main lobby once the power came back — just to make sure everything was okay — and she was in the corner with that big dude she's dating. Seriously, he's like the Hulk or some-thing he's so big."

"I could take him in a fight," Quinn noted. "He's not that big."

"Who said anything about a fight?"

Rowan arched a challenging eyebrow. "Yeah. Who said anything about a fight?"

"I was just saying that he's not as big as he looks," Quinn countered. "It's not as if he's a giant or something."

"Right," Demarcus said knowingly. "He's not a giant. I thought you two were copacetic? I saw you sitting out here talking for more than an hour today. You seemed to be getting along, sharing war wound stories and everything."

"How do you know what we were sharing?" Quinn asked.

"I'm an eavesdropper. Sue me."

Quinn scowled. "We were simply getting to know one another."

"Oh, it was a man date, huh?" Demarcus winked at Rowan, causing her to giggle. "I think that's a good idea. You don't have nearly enough man dates."

"Ugh. I don't even know why I try to talk to you sometimes."

"I think you're a glutton for punishment." Demarcus flicked his eyes back to Rowan. "Anyway, the Bohemian princess seemed to be upset about something. The Hulk was petting her hair and hugging her. I couldn't hear what they were saying, but they headed toward the elevator instead of the dining room. I think the power outage shook her for some reason, but it seems like an extreme reaction."

"It does seem like an extreme reaction," Rowan agreed. "Still, maybe she's sick or something. I'm sure it's nothing to worry about."

"Do I look worried?" Demarcus tapped the edge of her glass. "Do you want another one or are you going to play it safe?"

"I think one is more than enough for me."

"I knew you would play it safe."

"I think he's calling me a prude," Rowan complained to Quinn, causing him to smile.

"I happen to like my prude," Quinn said. "Finish up your drink and we'll grab some dinner before it gets too late. Then we need to make a plan about how we're going to handle things tomorrow."

"Yes, sir."

"I know you think that annoys me, but you're wrong. It kind of turns me on."

"Well then ... ." Rowan took a deep drink. "What are your orders, sir?"

"Yup. That definitely turns me on."

IVY DIDN'T EAT MUCH BEFORE slipping into an uneasy sleep. She curled into Jack's side as he watched television and listened to the storm rage outside.

It was a doozy.

Living in northern Lower Michigan meant that thunderstorms were relegated to the summer months. Occasionally, if things got really bad during the winter, they were graced with something called "thunder snow." Jack didn't believe it was a thing until he witnessed it himself. Still, huge thunderstorms weren't common in Shadow Lake. For some reason, though, on the open sea, this one was almost soothing.

He kept the volume on the television low, old reruns of *Friends* running in the background. Ivy picked at the dish she ordered from room service, but it mostly went to waste. Jack ate an entire steak and both of his sides before joining Ivy in bed.

Whatever she saw in the vision — or whatever it was — jolted her. She was subdued for the rest of the night, her mind clearly busy, and no matter how Jack tried to cajole her out of her mood, she was determined to remain in her own little world. Ultimately he gave up, tucked her in at his side, and was relieved when she drifted off to sleep. That gave him a chance to think about things without her watching his every facial expression for a hint.

In truth, Ivy's abilities had been growing since they met. When things first started, she had a hint of intuition that he found intriguing. He wasn't even sure she realized she had it. She simply knew the best way to approach things, where to look, and how to react when certain situations arose.

Things got weird when they started sharing dreams. Ivy claimed Jack called to her in his slumber, which he believed, but she supplied the power to make it happen. Somehow she sensed he needed her to break from the endless string of nightmares that haunted him. The dreams they shared weren't always nightmares. Now that he'd put the past behind him, they shared fun dreams. They went on dates ... and she wore coconut bras to amuse him. They fished, something she would never do in real life because she refused to harm an animal. Sometimes they camped, although it was much better than their real camping trip. Still, Jack made a mental note to set up a camping trip for the summer. Ivy loved camping, which meant he would learn to tolerate it.

No matter how weird the dreams were, they weren't the end of it. She'd seen through the eyes of a killer, which made her a potential victim. They'd solved that case together, but it had been scary toward the end. She'd also talked to a ghost, a feat she accomplished a second time around when hanging with a ghost hunter, and she'd managed to convey her fear to him on more than one occasion.

Jack didn't believe for a second he was psychic. Ivy was supplying all of the power for the things she managed to accomplish. However she was accomplishing it, though, it was never by design. She didn't set out to do any of the magical things she managed ... except for the dream walking. They made regular dates for that, although not too many because they both agreed that tripping into each other's heads every night probably wasn't smart or healthy.

Ivy murmured something at his side, cuddling closer.

Jack stared at her for a long time, making sure she remained settled, and then he tucked in the covers around her before killing the television and the light. He slouched a little lower in the bed, securing his arm around her back so she would feel safe, and closed his eyes.

They hadn't agreed to dream walk tonight, but somehow he knew she would be waiting for him. Once he fell into slumber, he knew exactly where he would find her, and he wasn't disappointed. She was working in the garden in front of the house they shared, seemingly intent on some task he didn't fully understand.

"Why are you here?" Jack asked, causing her to look over her shoulder. "We should be doing something fun."

"I wasn't sure you were coming tonight."

"I wouldn't give up the opportunity to spend time with you for anything."

"Oh, so sweet." Ivy abandoned her trowel and removed her work gloves. It wasn't necessary to wear gloves in a dream, but she always did. She was a stickler for certain rules. "Do you want to go to the fairy ring with me?"

Her fairy ring, located in the woods that surrounded the cottage, was her favorite spot when the weather allowed a visit. It was peaceful, and the one place she could always relax.

"That sounds great." Jack extended his hand. "We'll go to the fairy ring and have a picnic since you didn't get to eat very much tonight."

"I'm not hungry."

"And yet a picnic still sounds fun, doesn't it?" As if by magic, a basket appeared in his hand. "It's your favorite cucumber sandwiches. I also packed a pound of chocolate."

Ivy snorted, amusement washing over her. "That was impressive. You're learning how to control the dreamscape."

"You would be surprised by what I can learn when it comes to making you happy."

"Well ... I'm sorry about tonight. I didn't mean to ruin an entire evening of our vacation."

"You don't ruin things. Ever. This is just as good as walking around the ship."

"Are you sure?"

"Honey, when I'm with you, I'm sure about everything. You're my heart."

"You're mine, too."

"So, a picnic it is. Then I wouldn't mind a nice romp under the sun."

Ivy chuckled. "I like how you just put it out there without being embarrassed or anything."

"I believe in being honest."

"And that's why we're perfect for each other."

"Definitely."

TWELVE

I vy slept hard and was bright-eyed when she woke the next morning. Jack stretched as he watched her, enjoying the soft curve of her mouth.

"That was quite the dream last night," she offered, her smile wide.

"It was," he agreed. "I think you really liked those brownies I packed. And the chocolate."

Ivy snorted. "Yes. You must have spent hours slaving over a hot stove to bake those brownies."

"Don't hate the chef."

"I'm not hating the chef. I'm simply hungry." Her stomach growled loud enough to fill the room. "See."

"Then it's time for breakfast." He gave her a quick kiss. "I'm glad your appetite is back. As for the rest of it, we'll figure it out. I'm not sure why you saw what you saw, but we'll find answers. I promise."

"You always keep your promises, so I'll take it."

QUINN GROWLED WHEN HIS phone beeped on Rowan's nightstand, cursing under his breath when he snagged the phone.

Rowan stirred next to him, her auburn waves standing out in a hundred different directions.

"What's wrong?" she murmured as his jaw set. "Did something happen?"

"Unfortunately, yes. Emily Little."

"What about her?"

"She's dead."

Rowan bolted to a sitting position, her eyes going wide. All traces of sleep vacated her expressive face as her mouth dropped open. "Are you kidding me?"

"I don't generally find death funny." Quinn tossed off the covers and got to his feet, searching the floor for the clothes he discarded the previous evening. They were still damp from walking in the rain, and wrinkled. "I need to run back to my room. I'm going to take a quick shower. My guys photographed the body right away, but since it was on deck, it's already been moved to the infirmary."

Rowan was stunned. "I don't understand."

"I don't either. Yet. I need to get down there, though." He shifted his eyes to her. "There's no need for you to hurry. You should take your time, get some breakfast. I'll be in touch as soon as I can."

Rowan wasn't thrilled with the suggestion, but she understood his job responsibilities took precedence this morning. "Okay. I'll come down after breakfast if you don't find me. I ... do you know how it happened?"

"Just that she was found on the deck this morning. I don't know about cameras ... or how she died ... or anything else. I have to go, sweetie."

"Then go." Rowan leaned forward and gave him a quick kiss. "This isn't your fault. You couldn't have known this was coming. In fact ... I didn't even think to look at photos of her yesterday. This is probably my fault."

"Don't say that." Quinn extended a warning finger. "You're not to blame for this. I'm not to blame either. I know that. Still, I'm chief of security. I can't help wondering if there was something I could've done to stop this."

"Like what?"

"I don't know. I need answers before I can start the flogging."

"Get the answers and skip the flogging. I'll check my photos."

"Okay. Be safe."

"You, too. I love you."

"Right back at you."

ROWAN OPTED FOR THE main dining room rather than the employee cafeteria. She had special privileges thanks to her job — she often had to take photos during meals — so she had more options than the rest of the staff. Even though she didn't mind the cafeteria, she wasn't in the mood to answer the questions she was positive would be flung from a hundred different directions by curious workers. Instead, she showered and dressed for a day of work, and hit the main dining room. She had every intention of eating alone ... until she saw Ivy and Jack sitting at a table.

She made up her mind on the spot, filling her plate with eggs, hash browns, sausage, and toast before heading in their direction.

They seemed deep in conversation, and for a moment Rowan wondered if she should leave them be. The notion of eating alone didn't appeal to her, though, and she was more interested in discovering if Demarcus had been right about their behavior during the storm.

"Do you mind if I join you?"

Jack looked up first. "Of course not." His smile as friendly. "How are you this morning?"

"I've been better." Rowan poured herself a mug of coffee from the carafe at the center of the table. She took a long drink before continuing, losing her train of thought when she realized she wasn't drinking coffee. "What is this?"

"Tea," Ivy answered. "I don't like coffee."

"And I've gotten used to the tea so I can go either way," Jack supplied. "You look tired. Did you have a late night?"

"The power outage threw everyone," Rowan explained, taking another sip of the tea and deciding it wasn't so bad. "There's caffeine in this, right?"

"Definitely." Ivy bobbed her head. "Even I can't live without caffeine."

"She's evil without caffeine," Jack corrected. "She gets mean and growls. I can't even talk to her most mornings until she's two cups deep."

"That is a gross lie," Ivy argued.

Rowan smiled at their banter. "You guys seem happy this morning. I wasn't sure if you would be. I heard you were upset last night, Ivy. That's one of the reasons I wanted to check on you."

Ivy's eyebrows hopped. "You heard I was upset? How?"

"Demarcus saw you. He's the bartender at the tiki bar. He was caught outside when the power went out. I guess even the deck lights died, which is kind of freaky to think about. When the lights came back on, he headed inside. He said you guys were in the lobby and you looked upset."

"Oh, well ... ." Ivy wasn't sure how to respond.

"I'm claustrophobic," Jack answered automatically. "I know it seems weird to say because we were in the dining room, and it's huge, but when the lights went out, I felt as if I was being smothered. I needed to get away from all the people. Ivy was simply worried about me."

Even though she was grateful Jack was quick on his feet when thinking up an excuse, Ivy wasn't entirely comfortable with the lie. "I felt a little claustrophobic, too," she admitted, rueful. "I'm used to wide open spaces. When the power goes out in Shadow Lake, I don't always notice because it's dark around the house anyway. It was so weird last night."

"You're telling me." Rowan enthusiastically sawed into her sausage. "I've been on this ship for months and that's never happened, and I've been in the middle of some pretty terrific storms. I thought maybe I was overreacting, but Quinn has been stationed here a lot longer than me and it was a first for him."

"Where is Quinn?" Jack asked, doing his best to appear casual. "Is he continuing his investigation?"

Rowan momentarily forgot Quinn's competition with Jack and

shook her head. "No, we had another body this morning. He's off dealing with that."

Ivy placed her feet flat on the floor as she leaned closer. "What?"

Rowan realized what she said too late. "Oh, um ... you can't tell anyone." She felt like an idiot. "I shouldn't have told you. Quinn is not going to be happy when he finds out."

"We won't tell him," Ivy said hurriedly. "You have my word. Who died?"

"Emily Little."

"She was Margaret Adkins's assistant, right?" Jack queried. "I remember her name. She was young, blond, and kind of bubbly."

"I didn't spend a lot of time with her, but that's pretty much how I would describe her," Rowan agreed. "She was the one who found Margaret's body."

"How did she die?"

"I don't know. Quinn didn't really know. His guards found her on the deck this morning. There's protocol in situations like that. They have rules they absolutely have to follow, like quickly photographing the scene and calling for the medical staff so they can immediately take her away. Quinn didn't get the call until they'd already moved her body. They had to be quick."

"I don't understand." Jack struggled to keep himself in check. "Why did they have to move the body so quickly? Why not simply cordon it off?"

"Because I can't think of anyone who would want to hang out on the deck while a dead body was laying a few feet away," Rowan replied. "Plus the weather — the heat and humidity — can cause a body to break down quickly. Quinn taught me that."

"They didn't move Margaret Adkins immediately," Ivy pointed out.

"Because she was in her room," Jack surmised. "They could control the scene by simply closing the door and keeping out looky-loos that way. Plus, the rooms are air-conditioned."

"Pretty much," Rowan agreed. "I honestly shouldn't have told you about Emily. I don't know if her travel companions have been informed yet. I don't know anything other than the brief update Quinn got before leaving this morning."

"And where is he now?" Jack asked.

"The infirmary."

"And where was the body found?" Ivy asked, causing Jack to give her a slant-eyed look. "You said she was on the deck. Do you happen to remember where?"

"I believe it was on the port side."

"Which is what direction?" Jack asked.

"Um ... west. Yeah, it would be the west side."

Ivy drummed her fingers on the table as she considered the statement. She couldn't help but wonder if Emily Little was the same woman she caught a glimpse of in the vision when the power went out. "Do you know when she died?"

Jack, practically reading her mind, rested his hand on top of hers. "Was it during the blackout?"

"I hadn't even considered that." Rowan straightened in her chair. "Huh. I don't know. I wondered how she was killed on the deck without anyone noticing, even during a storm, but the blackout would've made decent cover."

"Definitely." Jack was thoughtful as he squeezed Ivy's fingers. "I hope you find who is doing this."

"Quinn will." Rowan was certain of that. "He doesn't fail. Never."

"I hope his streak continues."

ROWAN FINISHED HER BREAKFAST, held a brief conversation with Ivy and Jack before they headed to the pool to relax, and then made her way to the infirmary. She wasn't surprised to find a "closed" sign on the door. Potential patients were instructed to ring a bell if they needed help, which is exactly what Rowan did.

The nurse who opened the door looked confused. "Are you sick?"

"No. I'm here to see Quinn."

"He's busy."

"I know he's busy." Rowan tugged on her limited patience. "I'm here to help him with his problem."

"Are you suddenly part of his security staff and nobody told me?"

Rowan wasn't familiar with the nurse, but she didn't like the woman's attitude. "I'm here to take photos of the body." That was a total lie. She had no intention of snapping photographs of Emily Little's lifeless body. She did, however, have a desperate need to see Quinn.

The nurse let loose a long-suffering sigh. "I'll have to ask him if it's okay. Wait here." She pointed at the spot where Rowan stood for emphasis. "Right there. Don't try to sneak in."

Rowan worked at controlling her temper as the door shut. She had no idea how long she should wait before ringing the bell again. Ultimately, it didn't matter. This time when the door opened, Quinn was on the other side.

"I wasn't sure I was going to be allowed inside."

Quinn managed a wry smirk. "I don't think Desiree wanted you to come inside."

"Desiree?" Rowan furrowed her brow. "Is that the annoying nurse's name?"

Quinn nodded. "She has a crush on me. Don't let it get to you."

"Who doesn't have a crush on you?"

Amused despite the serious situation, Quinn shrugged. "I only care that you have a crush on me." He absently ran his hand up and down her arm. "Not that I'm not happy to see you, but what are you doing here?"

"I checked my photos." Rowan raised her camera for emphasis. "There's no omen in Emily's photos. I double and triple checked. We couldn't have known it was going to happen."

Quinn realized Rowan needed that reassurance more than he did. "Well, that's something at least." He glanced at the photo she showed by way of proof. "There's nothing. That probably means she was killed on a whim, huh? There was no premeditation involved."

"That would be my guess. I know she was found on the port side of the ship. Can you tell me anything about the scene?"

"Not much. She was strangled — this time with bare hands — and left out in the storm. That probably washed away all trace elements, but we're looking anyway. The doctor is putting her death at around nine or so, but it's hard to get a definitive timeline."

"Nine? That was during the blackout."

"Yeah, I figured that out, too." Quinn motioned for Rowan to move to the far corner of the room with him so they could converse without bothering the medical team working on Emily's body. Desiree, who stood close to the doctor and handed him various medical implements, openly glared at Rowan.

"She really does have a crush on you, huh? Am I going to have to fight her?"

"You're perfectly safe in my love," Quinn teased. "She's just ... being difficult. The staff here isn't used to working on dead bodies very often. They usually get bumps and bruises, the occasional broken arm, and in very rare instances a heart attack or stroke. Two dead bodies in two days puts everyone on edge. Don't take it personally."

"I'll try not to. Although, if she keeps glaring at me that way, I'm totally going to smack her around."

Quinn impulsively hugged Rowan, chuckling lightly into her hair. "I love that you always know how to make me feel better, even in the most difficult circumstances."

"Yeah. I'm a real prize." She patted his back before separating. "Have you checked the cameras? Do we know who was on the deck with her last night?"

"No. The cameras were down because of the blackout."

"Oh." Realization dawned on Rowan. "Are we sure the storm took down the electrical grid?"

"I've been wondering that myself." Quinn rubbed the back of his neck. "It seems a little too convenient. The thing is, I don't know how anyone could've managed to shut off the power. It seems to me that Emily's death was in the moment because the omen didn't show up in the photos. It would've taken a plan — an extensive one — to kill the power."

"So you're working under the assumption that whoever killed Emily took advantage of the blackout to do it, and not vice versa."

"Pretty much," Quinn confirmed. "It was dark out there. Demarcus said Emily was in the Neptune Bar at some point before the blackout. I'm going to need to pin down a timetable with him. From the sounds of it, she was tipsy. She came up to the deck, probably with someone she knew, and was killed."

"But why? What's the motive? I can see why someone would want to kill Margaret Adkins. That doesn't mean it's right, of course, but I can see why someone would want to do it. She wasn't well liked and she was messing with people's livelihoods. Emily was a simple assistant, though. I'm not even sure she was a true believer in the cause."

"I don't know what to tell you." It was early in the day, but Quinn already felt weariness weighing on him. "I can't figure out motives either. I'm going to wait until the doctor is finished with his exam. Then I'm getting a list of people who were at the bar with Emily last night. I'll go from there."

"Do you want any help?"

"From who? Desiree? I'll have to think about it."

Rowan playfully twisted his thumb. "Do you think that's funny?"

"I think it's funny that you're jealous."

"I am not jealous."

"Close enough." He kissed the tip of her nose, earning a double glare from Desiree. "You can come with me if you want when I start the questioning. I figure you need to take shots, though, too. Otherwise you might get in trouble."

"I think I can balance both."

"Then we'll work together. In fact, if you could take photos of everyone in that little group, that would be great. If someone else is slated to die, I would like to get ahead of it."

Rowan nodded, her stomach twisting. "I'll do my best."

"You always do."

THIRTEEN

R owan returned to the deck to take photos. She snapped everyone in the National Organization for Clean Minds and Hearts that she could find. It wasn't difficult, because those in charge had grouped together in an isolated spot.

She snapped a bevy of photos before moving to the tiki bar, purposely picking a table that was behind a small wall so she wouldn't be disturbed as she stared at the snapshots. She took her time, scanning each photo in its entirety, and came up empty. The symbol wasn't on any of the photos.

She couldn't decide if that was a good or bad thing.

What she didn't immediately realize was that Ivy and Jack were also in the tiki bar, squirreled away on the other side of the wall so they could talk in private. Once they started talking, though, she recognized their voices ... and couldn't stop herself from listening.

"I found out where the body was discovered," Jack offered, his voice low. "It was here. I took a photo on my phone."

Ivy took the phone and stared at the view it offered, silent.

"Is that the spot you saw in your head last night?" he prodded.

Rowan stirred on the other side of the wall, intrigued. She had no idea what they were talking about, but something sparked in her own head given the way Jack phrased the statement. Ivy saw things in her head? How? Why? What did she see?

"I don't know, Jack," Ivy replied. "The ship looks the same to me from almost every angle."

"Maybe we should head over there and take a look around. Something might ignite your memory."

"Except I didn't see anything of note." Ivy's voice was tinged with frustration. "I told you. All I saw was the deck railing."

"You felt something, though." Jack wasn't about to let it go. "You saw things from someone else's perspective. You felt fear."

"And now a woman is dead," Ivy shot back. "I should've done something last night. This is my fault."

"Don't say that." Jack was edgy as he shifted on his chair, his eyes hard. "You didn't kill her. You're not to blame for this. Besides, this is different from before. How could you possibly know who was in trouble? How were you supposed to know how to help?"

"I should've figured it out." Ivy was morose as she rubbed her forehead. "That girl was young. She didn't need to die."

"Well, you didn't kill her. I don't like the idea of you blaming yourself for this."

"Who else should I blame?"

"The person who killed her."

"Ugh." Ivy lowered her forehead to her palm and rubbed. "I'm getting a headache."

Sympathy rolled over Jack as he patted her free hand. "Maybe you should go back to the room, take a nap."

Ivy immediately started shaking her head. "No. We need to find the spot where her body was discovered. You were right. Maybe I'll recognize something ... or seeing it will jar something else in my head."

Jack wasn't sure he wanted that to happen. Now that he could see up close how she was being worn down, he wanted to protect her. They were supposed to be on vacation, after all. "Honey, we don't have to be a part of this." He chose his words carefully. "We're on vacation. This isn't our problem."

"I saw her, Jack. I felt her. It might not be your problem, but it's mine."

"Don't say that. Your problems are my problems."

Ivy was rueful. "Are you starting to regret taking me on?"

"No. I'm starting to regret leaving the room. We should've spent the entire time living on love and room service."

"We could've done that at home."

"Good point." He lifted her hand and pressed a kiss to the palm. "Come on. There's no sense putting it off. We'll head over there together. If nothing happens, then I say we put this behind us and move on."

Ivy wasn't sure that was possible. "I felt her fear, Jack."

He sighed. "We'll take it one step at a time. Finish your iced tea and then we'll head over there. We need to be careful so nobody sees us. The last thing I want is a bunch of unnecessary questions from Security Chief Stick-Up-His-Butt."

Ivy snorted. "He's not so bad. I kind of like him."

"That's because he's not trying to prove his superiority over you."

"He has a job to do."

"Apparently, so do we." Jack held out his hand. "Come on, honey. Let's get this over with."

Rowan waited until she was certain they'd moved away from the table to lean back and stare around the wall. She could see them moving across the desk, fingers linked, and her brain was moving a mile a minute.

"What the heck was that?"

ROWAN FOUND QUINN IN HIS office twenty minutes later. She expected him to be questioning members of the group. Instead, he appeared to be looking over a manifest.

"What are you doing?" Rowan entered without knocking, securing the door behind her.

"What are you doing?"

"Looking for you."

"Oh, yeah?" Quinn leaned back in his chair, stress lines creasing his forehead. "If you're here to tell me more bad news, I'm not sure I can take it."

"I'm here to tell you a few things." Instead of sitting in one of the chairs across from his desk, Rowan moved behind Quinn and massaged his shoulders. "I think you've had a rough morning, though. Do you want to tell me about your day first?"

"Oh, that feels amazing." Quinn closed his eyes and enjoyed the way her hands moved across his back. "Seriously, sweetie, that is ... awesome."

Rowan smiled as she glanced at the top of his head. "I aim to please."

"And you do. A little lower."

Rowan gladly acquiesced. "What did the doctor say?"

"She was strangled. He managed to scrape some DNA from under her fingertips, but we have no way of matching it until we have a suspect. I doubt the other members of the group are going to voluntarily give us their DNA."

"Probably not," Rowan agreed. "Although ... I saw this thing on television once. The police ran DNA tests off discarded cigarettes and chewing gum. Maybe we can do something like that."

Quinn knew better than to laugh at her, but he couldn't help himself. "Oh, you're so cute I can't stand it. I mean it."

"I was being serious."

"I know. That's what makes you even cuter."

"Tell me why that's not a good idea."

"Because there's no smoking allowed on the ship and most people don't simply toss gum on the ground when there are trash receptacles at every corner."

"Oh." Rowan's hope deflated. "I didn't even think about that."

"That's okay." He patted her stilled hand. "You can make it up to me by continuing to rub me until I purr."

Even though she was disappointed with her own narrow-minded idea, Rowan snorted and went back to the massage. "Did the doctor say anything else? Can he narrow the suspect field to male or female?"

"Actually, no. The hands used to strangle her weren't overly large. That means it could go either way. We might know more if we could test the DNA, but we don't have those capabilities on the ship."

"Well, that's a bummer."

"No doubt."

Rowan pursed her lips. "So, what are you doing in here?"

"Running the names of the people in the group who were in the block of rooms close to Margaret. I'm trying to see if I can find anyone with a less-than-savory background."

"Anything good?"

"Well, I found Mark Denton. He joined the group about a year ago. He moved up fast through the ranks. From what I can tell, he handles the website and online content."

"And what did you find in his background that set your Spidey senses into overdrive?"

"He's been arrested and charged three times. Once for drunk driving, once for drugs, and once for frequenting a drug house."

Rowan furrowed her brow, confused. "That doesn't sound like the sort of guy who would be helping run a campaign like this one."

"That's what I thought," Quinn agreed. "He's definitely on my list for interviews this afternoon. I mean ... it's possible he cleaned up his act and turned his life around. Maybe he joined the church and they pointed him toward this group. It's possible."

"But you don't believe it."

"I don't know what I believe."

"Well, not to add to your problems, but have you considered that maybe the killer isn't part of the group?"

"What do you mean?"

"Maybe whoever killed Margaret didn't want to join the group, or perhaps couldn't for other reasons, and instead found out about the cruise and signed up as a regular guest," Rowan replied. "Maybe he simply flew under the radar, perhaps talked himself into Margaret's room the night she died, and then slipped back under the radar."

"Okay, but why go after Emily?"

"Maybe she saw him at some point and he was worried she would squeal."

"Emily said she didn't see anyone hanging around Margaret, though."

"Yes, but she was in shock from seeing the body that way. She might've remembered more when her memory cleared."

"I guess." Quinn rubbed his chin before jiggling his shoulders. "I don't think you're quite done rubbing me yet."

Amused, Rowan went back to her task. "I took the photos you wanted, by the way. The omen isn't there. I went through everything I had ... twice. The omen never showed up on Emily's photos and it doesn't appear on any of the other photos I took of the group."

"That's a good thing, isn't it?"

Rowan didn't answer, causing Quinn to turn in his chair so he could study her face. "Isn't it?" he prodded.

"Normally I would say yes. Emily didn't have the omen, though. I don't understand why that is. The omen always shows up."

Quinn opted to be pragmatic. "You said it yourself. It could've been a heat-of-the-moment attack. Most of the time, we have a little notice to deal with these things. That can't always be the case."

"I guess."

Quinn reached around and grabbed Rowan, tugging her to his lap so he could wrap his arms around her and kiss her cheek. "Don't beat yourself up about this. I don't like it. Not even a little. You're better than this."

"I feel kind of helpless. When your nurse girlfriend Desiree asked why I thought I was part of the team this morning, I was angry. Maybe she had a point."

"Oh, don't turn all melancholy. I hate that." He pressed another kiss to her cheek. "I love you. You're part of the team no matter what, and it's not simply because of the omens. You're good on your feet and you think things through in a logical manner. I like that about you."

"That kind of sounds like code for being boring."

"You're so far from boring you don't even live on the same continent."

"That's nice of you to say."

"I meant it."

"Good." Rowan exhaled heavily as she rested her head against his cheek. "There's one other thing I have to tell you."

"Uh-oh." Quinn braced himself. "The fact that you kept it for last worries me."

"I don't know how you should feel about it. Truly."

"Okay, tell me what it is and we'll go from there."

"I was in the tiki bar and I happened to overhear a conversation."

"Was it about murder?"

"Not quite." Rowan related Jack and Ivy's conversation to Quinn. Part of her felt guilty about it — she knew she would be upset if someone shared her secret — but she was in over her head and needed help puzzling things out. "So, basically, I think that symbol on her photo means something else entirely."

Quinn had no idea what to make of what Rowan told him. "I don't understand," he said finally. "Are you saying she's psychic?"

"I think that's probably the easiest way to state it. It sounded to me like she saw something in her head last night, and that something tied into what happened to Emily."

"Huh." Quinn was legitimately stumped. "Maybe that symbol was supposed to tip you off that someone like you was close."

"I don't think she's like me," Rowan argued. "I'm not psychic."

"You see death and danger omens in photographs, sweetheart. If that's not at least partially psychic, I don't know what is."

Rowan frowned. "I'm honestly not psychic. I don't think you can use that word to describe me."

"Okay." He absently patted Rowan's thigh. Now wasn't the time to argue about her abilities. They could save that for another day. "Demarcus said he saw them in the lobby last night and Ivy looked upset. He said Jack was trying to comfort her. That must have been after the blackout."

"Right."

"The doctor believes Emily died during the blackout. The timing is right."

"So ... oh." Realization dawned on Rowan. "Ivy and Jack are working on the assumption that Emily died after the vision ... or whatever it was. They don't know the time of death."

"They don't know that Ivy was probably seeing the death as it happened," Quinn said, making his decision on the spot. He gave Rowan a smacking kiss on the cheek and pushed her to a standing position. "Come on. We need to find them."

Rowan was taken aback. "What are you going to do when you find them?"

"Have a chat."

"But ... what if they deny everything?"

"Then they deny everything. We still need to talk to them. Come on." He grabbed her hand and gave her a light tug. "There's no sense in putting it off."

"IS THIS THE SPOT?"

Ivy rubbed the back of her neck as she studied the deck space Jack indicated. They'd taken up position a good thirty feet away so they wouldn't look suspicious while studying the deck. That didn't stop Ivy from feeling awkward and out of place.

"That's the spot," Jack confirmed, rubbing his hand over her slim back. "Do you recognize anything?"

"I'm not sure." Ivy chewed on her lip as she slowly swiveled, narrowing her eyes when she caught sight of the door behind them. "Does that open?"

"It's a door."

"You know what I mean. Is it locked?"

Jack chuckled at her withering tone. "There's only one way to find out." He strolled to the door and gave it a firm tug. It opened without complaint, and when Ivy peered inside, she nodded without hesitation.

"This is the hallway she was running through," Ivy said. "That painting right there, the one of the lighthouse in the storm, I recognize it. Someone was chasing her, she burst through this door, and ran onto the deck."

"What was she feeling at the time?"

"Terrified."

"Look beyond that, honey," Jack prodded. "She was feeling more than one thing, right? She was thinking more than one thing. Try to remember."

Ivy closed her eyes and swayed back and forth, searching her memory of the vision. "She was surprised. She didn't know she was in trouble until it was already too late."

"That's good." Jack kept his voice low and soothing. "Can you get a picture of who was chasing her?"

"No."

"Man or woman?"

"I don't know."

"Okay, don't push that right now," Jack said. "What happened when she hit the deck? Did she run straight to the railing or did she try to escape in another direction first?"

"I don't think she was thinking about that either way. She was surprised when she hit the deck and realized it was storming. The only reason she recognized how isolated she was is because of the lightning. It was dark, no deck lights or anything. The only illumination came from the storm."

"Okay."

"She was terrified, and discombobulated," Ivy continued. "She tripped over a lounger, banged her shin in the process. It hurt." Ivy absently leaned over and rubbed her shin, something Jack didn't like because he wasn't keen on her putting herself into the mind of a woman who died.

"She just ran forward because she didn't know what else to do," Ivy said finally. "She was caught in front of the railing. It was too dark to see the person she was fighting with. She fought hard to breathe, so hard it burned. She couldn't see, though. She couldn't breathe. It hurt."

"That's enough of that." Jack grabbed Ivy's arm and pulled her to him. "You don't have to remember that. Not again. That's more than enough."

"Oh, I'm not sure about that."

Jack froze at the sound of the interrupting voice and turned, his eyes going dark when he found Rowan and Quinn staring at him from the open doorway he'd walked through with Ivy a few moments before. "What are you doing here?"

"I was just about to ask you the same thing," Quinn replied. "It's an awfully nice day to be hiding in a hallway."

"We're not hiding." Jack stroked Ivy's hair to calm her. "Ivy isn't used to the sun. She has extremely fair skin. We're taking a break."

"Uh-huh." Quinn didn't look convinced as he folded his arms across his chest. "Word on the ship is that your girlfriend is psychic and she saw something last night."

Rowan's mouth dropped open. "Quinn!"

He ignored her and barreled forward. "I'm dying to know what she saw. Dying being the operative word, of course."

"I have no idea what you're talking about," Jack lied, clutching Ivy closer to him. "We're simply taking a break from the sun. If someone told you Ivy is psychic ... well ... that's a load of crap. She's just a simple woman. She bakes barefoot and yells at me for not putting my laundry away. Does that sound like a psychic to you?"

"I'm not sure." Quinn's eyes shifted to Ivy and there was genuine sympathy reflected there when he took in Ivy's pale countenance. "I don't want to make things rough on you, but I'm not going to let this go. I think we need to talk."

Jack refused to back down. "There's nothing to talk about."

"I think there is."

"Well, I think ... ."

Ivy put her hand on Jack's arm to still him. "It's okay. We can talk to him. It's probably best that we do."

Jack wasn't convinced. "I'm not sure that's a good idea."

"And I'm not sure you have a choice," Quinn pressed. "It's either come with me now or come with me later ... when I gather my men to haul you in."

Jack scowled. "You're really starting to bug me."

"Right back at you."

14

FOURTEEN

Jack insisted Rowan and Quinn accompany him back to the VIP room. Quinn suggested his office, but Jack refused to cede control and let Quinn have home-field advantage. He linked his fingers with Ivy's, smiled at her questioning look, and reassured her with a soft whisper that everything would be okay.

He believed that ... if only because he was willing to do whatever it took to make sure that was true.

"Wow. Look at this room." Rowan had never seen one of the VIP lofts in person before. She was flabbergasted. "This is five times as big as my room ... and it's nice."

Quinn slid her a sidelong look and mustered a smile. "I'll arrange for us to take over one of these rooms for an upcoming cruise. You can get a taste of it firsthand."

"You don't have to do that. My room is ... okay."

"Yeah, well, maybe I want you to have the best." Quinn winked at her before turning serious and focusing on Ivy and Jack.

For their part, the antsy couple sat together on the couch so Jack could act as a buffer. The big man put his arm around Ivy's back, kissed her cheek, and refused to speak first. He left that task to Quinn.

"I understand something happened last night," Quinn started.

"Yes, the power went out," Jack drawled, adopting an imperious tone. "I'm considering writing the cruise line bigwigs to voice my disappointment. You can bet this little question-and-answer session will be included in that complaint as well."

Quinn blinked several times in rapid succession before speaking. "Why was Ivy upset last night?"

"She didn't like the offerings at dinner," Jack answered without hesitation.

"You ordered room service once you got back to the room, the same offerings available in the dining room."

"And she didn't eat what I ordered for her," Jack supplied. "If you're watching us closely enough to know that we left the dining room early, you probably checked the trays we left out for housekeeping, too, right?"

Quinn frowned. Actually, he hadn't bothered to collect a report on the empty trays. "I'm not really interested in what Ivy is eating."

"Well, I'm glad we got that cleared up." Jack slapped his knee and pointed toward the door. "You know the way out."

"We're nowhere near done here." Quinn's voice was even, chilly. "I want to know what Ivy saw last night."

"She saw a storm on the deck. She happens to love storms. Then we came back to the room and watched *Friends* before going to sleep."

"Oh, really?" Quinn cocked a challenging eyebrow. Jack's attitude bothered him to no end and he wanted to push the man to crack. "Which episode?"

"You want to know what episode we watched?" Jack matched Quinn jab for jab. "Well, let me see. I believe we watched the episodes where they compete for Monica and Rachel's apartment, Monica fixes up the other apartment, and something about Rachel having a date that's interrupted by the chicken and duck. Is that specific enough for you?"

Quinn frowned. He had no idea if those episodes really existed. He looked to Rowan for help, causing her to laugh.

"All those episodes are real," she said after a beat. "Why did you even ask if you didn't know the answer?"

"That's a very good question," Jack said. "I would like to hear the answer to it."

"I forgot some of the episodes," Quinn replied lamely. "That's hardly here nor there. I'm more interested in why you left the dining room. What did Ivy see as you were leaving?"

"It was dark." Jack managed to keep calm ... but just barely. "She didn't see anything. It was a tense walk out of the dining room because I was worried we would get separated in the crowd. She was upset because we're both a little claustrophobic."

"You're claustrophobic?" Quinn pressed. "You don't seem the type."

"You should try getting shot in the chest," Jack suggested. "When your lung won't inflate, you feel as if you're being crushed. I couldn't open my eyes. It was dark. I felt as if the world was closing in on me. So, yeah, I'm claustrophobic."

Quinn balked. "I'm sorry. I ... shouldn't have said that." He was sincere. Despite Jack's attitude, Quinn felt bad about questioning the couple. He didn't believe they were suspects, but there was something decidedly odd about both of them. Jack was determined to protect Ivy at all costs — something he understood because he felt the same way about Rowan — but Quinn was determined to get answers. "I didn't mean to insinuate you were lying."

"You did, though." Ivy's voice was small as Jack increased his hand movements on her back. "That's basically exactly what you said."

Rowan flicked her eyes to Ivy and frowned. "Quinn didn't mean to suggest Jack wasn't telling the truth."

"I can speak for myself, sweetie." Quinn awkwardly patted her hand. "As for what happened last night, various people saw you in the lobby after the fact. Ivy was described as pale and upset."

"She's claustrophobic, too," Jack said.

"It's weird for both halves of a couple to be claustrophobic."

"And yet that's what we live with day in and day out," Jack said. "If that's all, you can go."

"That's nowhere near all." Quinn's frustration bubbled up thanks to Jack's stonewalling efforts. "Listen, I don't know what's going on here, but I know Ivy gets visions." He blurted it out. "I know she saw something last night. All I want to know is what that something is."

Ivy sucked in a breath as Jack licked his lips.

"It's not a big deal," Rowan offered hurriedly. "If you have visions, I mean. I think it's kind of cool ... and understand that you probably conditioned yourself to keep it secret. You don't have to keep it secret from me."

Ivy kept her gaze focused on her lap. "I don't know what you're talking about."

"Ivy ... ." Rowan felt helpless. "I swear it's going to be okay if you tell me what's going on. I promise that we'll keep it a secret. You can trust us."

"Really?" Ivy finally lifted her chin, her anger coming out to play. "You think we can trust you, huh? You tracked us down on the deck, essentially threatened us, forced us to let you into our room so you could accuse us of keeping a ridiculous secret, and now you're badgering us with inane questions when we're supposed to be on vacation. You think we can trust you after that?"

Rowan's mouth dropped open. "Well, it doesn't sound so good when you phrase it like that."

"Don't yell at her," Quinn snapped. "She's not to blame for this. If you'd talked quieter in the tiki bar, she wouldn't have heard you in the first place."

Now Ivy was the one who couldn't hide her surprise. "You eavesdropped on us?"

"That's it." Jack swiftly got to his feet at the exact time Quinn did, their chests almost bumping as they squared off. "I want you out of our room." He practically growled the order.

"I'm chief of security," Quinn reminded him. "I have whatever jurisdiction I want on this ship. You can't stop me."

"No? What if I place a call to corporate? What if I go to the news media and tell them we were attacked because you and your girlfriend decided my fiancée was psychic? How ridiculous do you think you're going to look then?"

"Don't threaten me," Quinn warned. "I'll throw you in a cell for the rest of the trip if you say another word. Don't think I won't. I have the power and I'll enjoy wielding it."

"Don't do that," Ivy protested, her voice cracking. "Don't take him."

Jack turned to her, his fight with Quinn abandoned. "Honey, don't worry about that. He won't take me away."

"He won't," Rowan agreed, ignoring the harsh look Quinn shot her. "I won't let him. This has gotten out of hand. I wanted to have a calm conversation with you guys, not a screaming match."

"Then perhaps you shouldn't have spied on us over lunch," Jack spat as he returned to his sitting position next to Ivy. "Honey, I don't want you getting upset. I'm going to handle this. Don't worry about anything."

"What is she worried about in the first place?" Quinn challenged, his eyes narrowing. "Why are you suddenly positioning yourself as her great protector? From everything I've seen, she can take care of her herself."

"She's the strongest person I know," Jack agreed. "That doesn't mean I appreciate you attacking her."

"I'm not attacking her. I'm trying to understand what's going on."

Rowan worked her jaw as she stared hard at Ivy's rigid features. Suddenly, realization dawned ... and she felt like a blooming idiot. "Shut up."

Jack and Quinn continued sniping at one another as if they hadn't heard her.

"Shut up!" Rowan bellowed loudly enough to stop both men in mid-sentence. "This isn't about either of you." She leaned forward so she could stare directly into Ivy's eyes. The pink-haired woman was defiant, but Rowan understood what was necessary to move the conversation along. "Weird things happen to me sometimes, too."

Whatever she was expecting, that wasn't it. Ivy arched an eyebrow, surprised. "What do you mean?"

"You saw. Yesterday, when we were inside and you were taking a break from the sun, you saw my gift. I don't know that I would call it that, but others do so I've gotten in the habit. You saw my gift and know I'm different. It's okay that you're different, too."

Ivy licked her lips, unsure. "What gift?" she asked finally. "What gift are you talking about?"

"The symbols on the photographs," Rowan replied without hesitation, determined to prove she wasn't a threat to Ivy. "You saw the symbol on your own photograph. I don't even know what that symbol means. I've been trying to figure it out, but I'm at a loss.

"You saw the one on Margaret Adkins's photograph, too, though," she continued. "We talked about it. I said there was probably something wrong with the settings on the camera, but that wasn't true. I've been able to predict people's deaths with my camera since I was a kid. I think you can do something similar ... although maybe a little more impressive."

Ivy rubbed her forehead as Jack slid his arm around her waist. "Those symbols you showed me are magical, aren't they?"

"I don't know. I've never been able to get a firm answer on them."

"You said you can predict death in your photos," Jack interrupted. "If Ivy has a symbol on her photograph, does that mean she's going to die?" He looked worried. "Do I need to get her off this ship?"

"Her symbol is different," Rowan replied hurriedly. "I don't know what the symbol on her photograph means. My friend Sally is from New Orleans and she managed to identify two other symbols I see in my photographs. One is for death, the other for danger. Ivy's symbol is different. I showed it to Sally and she said it looked like a pagan symbol, one that means 'crone,' but she can't be for sure."

Jack's hand was gentle as he stroked the back of Ivy's head. "So ... she's not in danger?"

"I don't think so." Rowan opted for honesty. "I don't know what the crone symbol means. It's frustrating for you — I get that — but I don't know what to tell you. I don't know what the symbol means."

"I think I know what it means." Jack's expression softened as he met Ivy's gaze and gave her an encouraging smile. "I think it means she's a witch ... or close to it."

Quinn almost fell off his chair. "Excuse me? A witch?"

"I don't particularly like that word," Ivy hedged. "I don't use it. My aunt uses it. Felicity. She considers herself a witch and she can do a few things. You know, magical things."

"What kind of magical things?" Quinn asked. "Like ... can she turn people into toads?"

Ivy rolled her eyes. "No. She can read tarot cards and tea leaves. She can contact ghosts in seances. She can see auras. Those types of things."

"And what types of things can you do?" Rowan asked, intrigued despite herself. "I heard you guys. I know you see things. I know you saw something last night and you're convinced it was Emily Little's death. I don't want to spread your secret far and wide. I would like to understand, though."

Ivy sighed, resigned.

"You don't have to." Jack collected her hand and gave it a squeeze. "You don't have to say anything you don't want to say."

"She told me her secret," Ivy pointed out. "It only seems fair."

Jack leveled a dark gaze on Quinn. "If you use this against her ... ."

Quinn held his hands up in capitulation. "I won't use this against her. Do you think I don't understand about wanting to protect the woman you love? I get it. You're doing this for her."

"I *am* doing this for her," Jack agreed. "I'll do whatever it takes to protect her."

"You don't have to protect her from me."

"You'd better hope not."

Ivy let loose a weary sigh as she leaned back in her seat. "I don't know what you would call me. I don't like the word 'witch,' but it might be the most apt one."

"What can you do?" Rowan asked.

"It started with dream walking."

"What's that?" Quinn queried, legitimately curious.

"We can share dreams," Jack replied. "It started not long after we met. We can pick a destination — good or bad — and go together."

"That sounds interesting." Quinn's eyes lit with excitement. "Do you go to exotic places?"

"Sometimes." Jack bobbed his head. "It didn't start with exotic locations, though. It started with a dirty alley in Detroit."

"Oh." Quinn was chagrined. "She helped you through what happened with your partner."

"I watched him almost die over and over again," Ivy corrected. "He figured a way out of there himself. He took me with him when he left."

"That sounds like a real bonding experience," Rowan encouraged.

"We definitely bonded early." Ivy mustered a wan smile for Jack. "There's been other things since then, though."

"Like what?"

"I saw through the eyes of a killer once, watched him work."

"That sounds less entertaining," Quinn said, shaking his head. "Is that it?"

"No." Ivy decided to lay everything out there. "I've had a few psychic visions, including popping into someone's head last night. I think it was Emily Little. She was being chased and I know she accessed the deck from the door you found us standing by a little while ago. I recognized that lighthouse painting ... unless there's more than one painting like that on the ship."

"No." Rowan emphatically shook her head. "I know the painting you're talking about. It's the only one I've seen on the ship. I know because I like it and always pay attention when I pass."

"There's something moody about it," Ivy agreed.

"Did you see who was chasing Emily?" Quinn asked. "Did you see a face? Or even a glimpse of hair or eyes."

"No. I've tried going back and accessing the memories. If Emily knew who was after her — and I'm pretty sure she did — she didn't share the information with me."

"Can you go deeper?" Quinn asked. "I mean ... can you do that dream-walking thing and go deeper to see what happened?"

"I don't think so." Ivy knew honesty was her only course of action, so she stuck with the truth. "I saw a flash. I thought I was seeing the future, that we would have more time. I can't control what I see, or feel. Sometimes it happens and I don't even realize it."

"She's called to me a few times when in danger," Jack volunteered. "She was in a grocery store before Christmas and someone wanted to hurt her. I instinctively knew where she was and which way to enter the store to save her. She showed me how to do it.

"There have been other times, too," he continued. "What happened last night was a first. We both assumed we had more time. If we'd known it was so imminent ... I don't know what we would've done. I would've tried to do something, though."

"I don't doubt that." Quinn turned weary as he rubbed his forehead. "Here's the thing, we believe that Ivy had the vision while the attack was happening. Demarcus said he saw you guys in the lobby right after the power came back on. The doctor puts Emily's time of death during the blackout. I don't happen to believe there was any way you could've stopped it."

"Really?" Ivy looked so hopeful it squeezed Jack's heart.

"Really," Quinn confirmed. "There was nothing you could've done."

"I believe I already told you that," Jack said. "How come you didn't believe me?"

Ivy gave him a rueful look. "Because you'll say whatever is necessary to make me feel better. Quinn doesn't have to say things like that unless they're true."

"I'm still better than him," Jack muttered under his breath, causing Ivy to let loose a legitimate smile.

Quinn decided to let the dig go. "I think we need to pool our resources. We have a better chance of figuring out what's going on if we work together."

"How do you expect to do that?" Ivy asked.

"You and Rowan have special abilities. I think, if you put your heads together, you might be able to come up with some answers."

"What about you?" Rowan pressed. "What are you going to do?"

"I'm going to keep investigating the only way I know how."

"You should have Jack help you with that," Ivy suggested, biting back a grin when Quinn frowned. "He's a police detective ... and very good at his job. If the two of you work together, you might figure things out faster."

"Oh, well, I don't know." Quinn held his hands palms out. "I don't want to ruin his vacation."

"I'm with Ivy," Jack interjected. "You can't ruin anything as long as I have her."

Something about Jack's tone stirred Quinn. He knew exactly how the other man felt. "Fine." He heaved out a sigh. "We'll all work together. We just need to figure out where to start."

"I have an idea on that," Rowan said. "Although ... I'm not sure you're going to like it."

FIFTEEN

The conversation was tense after Rowan and Ivy admitted to their abilities. For their part, the women were more curious than accusatory. The men, however, were determined to protect their women and became excessively agitated with one another.

"It seems to me that you guys should be able to figure out something together," Quinn started.

"That's easy for you to say," Jack muttered. "Your woman takes photos and then sits back to see if anything happens. My woman has to hop into heads of killers and victims and put herself on the line. That doesn't seem very balanced to me."

"Excuse me?" Quinn arched a challenging eyebrow. "What did you just say to me?"

"I believe he called me his woman," Ivy answered for Jack, her eyes darkening. "As if I'm property."

Jack wrinkled his nose. "Oh, don't pick a fight, honey. I'm not in the mood."

"Maybe I'm not in the mood," she challenged. "Have you ever thought of that?"

"And we're fighting about what again?"

Ivy stared him down. "I'm not your property."

"Fine." He held up his hands in capitulation. "You're not my woman. You're your own woman. I have no claims to you whatsoever."

"Oh, don't turn into a baby."

Rowan snickered as Ivy rolled her eyes. "You guys are funny."

"Yes, I often wear a red nose and do a clown dance," Jack drawled.

"While pounding his chest, pointing at me, and chanting 'mine, mine, mine,'" Ivy added, her annoyance obvious.

"Hey, we're getting married," Jack pointed out. "That means you're technically mine. Forever. You don't hear me complaining because I'm yours."

"I don't refer to you that way," Ivy pointed out. "I like to think we share two lives that often overlap. We choose to be together because we're mutually giving and loving individuals."

Jack stared at her a long beat. "That's a lovely sentiment."

Ivy beamed. "Thank you."

"I'll still hurt anyone who goes after you because you're mine," Jack said, earning an appreciative chuckle from Quinn.

Rowan narrowed her eyes as she glared at her boyfriend, who had the grace to be abashed and try to smother his laughter. "It's not funny."

"Of course not." Quinn straightened and sobered. "It's not funny at all. He's a complete and total Neanderthal. I'm embarrassed for him to be part of my gender."

"Thanks, man," Jack said dryly.

"Hey, it's every sexist jerk for himself."

Rowan scowled as she leaned back in her chair and stared at the ceiling. "I don't think you guys are helping our process," she said finally. "Don't you have something you can do ... elsewhere ... and leave us to discuss the important stuff?"

Jack immediately balked at the suggestion. "I'm not leaving Ivy."

"I'm perfectly fine," Ivy argued. "Besides, maybe it would be good for Rowan and me to have a chance to talk to one another alone. I mean ... we're the ones who are hiding our abilities. It's kind of a relief to be able to talk about it with someone who kind of understands."

Jack stared at her for a long beat. "I don't know. What if she hurts you?"

Quinn pinned him with a look. "How is she going to hurt Ivy? Rowan is a freaking angel."

"I don't doubt she's absolutely lovely," Jack shot back. "That doesn't mean I'm simply going to trust her because you say I should. Ivy is my heart. I'm not risking her for anything."

Ivy and Rowan slowly tracked their gazes to one another, heads shaking as lips curved.

"You know what?" Ivy said finally, recovering her wits. "I don't think it matters what either of you has to say about this. Rowan and I would like some time alone to discuss things. That means you guys can have some time alone to investigate ... whatever you feel like investigating."

Now it was Quinn's turn to make a face. "And what if I don't want him with me while we investigate?"

"You'll survive," Ivy replied simply. "He's good at his job and his instincts are solid."

"Thank you, honey." Jack beamed. "That, too, is a lovely sentiment. You left out the part where I'm the smartest cop in the world, though."

"Maybe that's because, as your woman, I can't think that far ahead without you," Ivy suggested, causing Jack's smile to slip.

"Oh, geez," he muttered, disgusted. "I'm never going to live this down, am I?"

"I don't know. Giving Rowan and me some time alone seems to be a good way to start working at it."

"Ah, so it's blackmail." Jack licked his lips and shifted his eyes to Quinn. "Do you need help with something?"

Quinn's sigh was long-suffering. "I'm sure I can find something for us to do."

"Then let's do it. Neither one of us is going to get what we want until they have some time alone together."

Quinn nodded, resigned. "I figured that out, too. Let's get out of here and spy on the group members. We might find some insight there."

"That sounds like a plan."

ONCE THE MEN DEPARTED, Ivy and Rowan had nothing to do but stare at each other. The room fell silent, their furtive gazes uncomfortable, and finally Rowan was the first to speak.

"I know you're worried I'm going to tell someone about your abilities, but that's not going to happen," she started. "I know what it's like to live with a secret. Granted, your secret is different from mine. They're not all that different, though. Not really."

"They feel different," Ivy hedged. "Tell me about the photos."

"What do you want to know?"

"How did you figure out what was happening?"

"I was young, in middle school," Rowan replied. "My father got me my first good camera. It was used because he didn't want to spend a lot of money if it was something I wouldn't continue with, but I was so excited when he gave it to me.

"I spent weeks snapping photographs of everything, random people on the street, you name it," she continued. "That included my teachers. One day, I saw the symbol and showed it to my father. He messed around with the camera, thinking there must be something defective about it, but couldn't find anything.

"Two days later, the man in the photo died," she said. "He was my principal and he passed away under mysterious circumstances. I was still young but heard my parents talking. His wife killed him when she caught him cheating ... with another student."

Ivy was horrified. "I don't usually wish ill on the dead, but you were in middle school. He had it coming."

Rowan snickered. "Yeah, well, we put the symbol behind us. Kind of forgot about it. We didn't know enough to put things together. Then it happened again with the lunch lady. Three days later she was dead. She was killed by her boyfriend for money."

"You must have been afraid," Ivy noted. "I think I would've been afraid."

"I was confused," Rowan corrected. "I didn't know what was happening. All I know is that it kept happening. We finally put things together, and after another two tests, my father realized I was able to predict certain deaths — murder, not natural causes — and we moved on from there."

"That's kind of freaky."

"You have no idea. I was terrified. Then my mother got sick and my father told me not to talk to her about what was happening because he didn't want to worry her. Then she died."

Ivy felt sick to her stomach. "I'm sorry. That must have been rough."

"It was. My father did his best to take care of me, though. He always was open for conversation. We talked things out. At first — and for a long time — it was only the one symbol. I thought that's all I would ever see."

"When did that change?"

"A few months ago," Rowan replied. "I saw another symbol, this one for danger. Then I saw the symbol on your photograph. I still don't know what to make of that. It didn't show up on the first photograph. It was only later when it appeared."

"Well, I tend to believe your theory that it showed up because I'm magical, too," Ivy said. "I'm still not used to that word. It makes me feel weird to use it."

"Me, too." Rowan smiled encouragingly. "I know what it's like to hide. I know what it's like to feel fear. You don't have to be afraid of me. I'll keep your secret, just like I trust you to keep mine."

Ivy sighed as she stared at the woman. "What do you want me to do?"

"First, I want to know exactly what you can do. After that, we'll start talking strategy."

"Fine. I don't know that you're going to be as excited as you think you're going to be when I tell you what I can do, though."

Rowan's eyes sparkled. "Try me."

"THEY DON'T SEEM ALL that broken up, do they?"

Jack and Quinn picked a spot at the tiki bar, in the shade and away from eavesdroppers, and watched the small group of National Organization for Clean Minds and Hearts talk at the center of the bar. They seemed to be having a good time, a lot of hearty guffaws and snickers, and were seemingly oblivious to the fact they were being watched.

"Yeah, I've been thinking the same thing since Margaret Adkins died," Quinn said, sipping his iced tea. "None of them were upset about her death. Emily was shaken because she found a dead body, but I didn't get the feeling that she cared all that much about her boss dying. Everyone I talked to basically said Margaret was a jerk."

"I found the same thing," Jack admitted, earning an annoyed look from Quinn. "What? Do you have a problem?"

"You're not supposed to be investigating my case," he replied sharply. "It's my case, like Ivy is your woman. By the way, it's perfectly normal to think those things. It's not normal to say them. You might want to learn discretion if you want to hold onto *your* woman."

Jack immediately started shaking his head. "I got exactly the reaction I was going for. Things are fine."

"And what reaction were you going for?"

"Ivy was uncomfortable, worried to the point where I thought she might make herself sick," Jack replied without hesitation. "She's not used to people finding out about her secret. She likes hiding her abilities. The only ones who know are her family, my partner, and me, for the most part. She likes it that way."

"So you basically poked her to get her looking at you instead of her fear, huh?" Quinn was outwardly impressed. "That was pretty smart."

"I know my woman." Jack's grin was light and easy. "She's going to be okay. This whole thing simply threw her for a loop. Once she settles, she'll be back to being feisty. She might even come up with a way for us to figure this all out."

Quinn traced the condensation on his iced tea glass. "You seem fine with what she can do. You're not freaking out or anything. I guess that means you're used to it, comfortable with it."

"There's no other way to be," Jack said simply. "I love her. I think I loved her from the first moment I laid eyes on her. I know that sounds ridiculous, but something chemical happened in my brain.

"I saw her and I wanted to take care of her," he continued. "She was barefoot at a crime scene. That's what sticks out to me most. She was barefoot and she yelled at me. I was a goner from that moment on."

Amused despite himself, Quinn chuckled. "I know what you mean. I felt the same way about Rowan. She was shyer, unsure of herself. This was a new adventure for her ... and she was all alone."

"No family?"

"It's hard to explain," Quinn hedged. "She technically has family, but she didn't at the time. I'm not sure she would want me talking about that, though."

"Fair enough." Jack held up his hands in capitulation. "I get it. You don't want to share her secrets out of turn."

"Exactly." Quinn bobbed his head. "What about Ivy? You're used to what she can do now. That dream-walking thing sounds interesting. Do you have fun with that?"

"We do." Jack's smile was huge. "We try to limit ourselves on the number of trips we take each week, though. We're both worried we'll spend too much time in the dreams and not enough time in the real world. That might lead to an inauthentic life. Neither of us wants that."

"That makes sense."

"Still, she does slip on the occasional coconut bra for me." Jack chuckled as Quinn rolled his eyes. "We also fish. Last night, I knew she was upset, so we visited her fairy ring together. That's where she goes when she's worked up at home. It centers her."

"What's a fairy ring?"

"Basically it's a circle of toadstools in the woods," Jack replied. "She discovered it when she was a kid and has always loved the location. When we're home and she goes missing, I almost always know where she's at."

"Does she care if you're out there with her?"

"No, but I make sure she has time to herself when she needs it. She was a solitary soul before I showed up on the scene. I was, too. We're building a life together, but we're both careful to recognize there are times when we still need space. I think we're both good that way."

"You really love her, don't you?"

Jack nodded without hesitation. "I had no idea it was possible to love anything as much as I love her. She takes over my soul when we're together, fills me with love. It's not just that I won't live without her. I can't. She's become my life."

Instead of rolling his eyes at the schmaltzy comment, Quinn simply nodded. "I feel that way about Rowan. When she arrived on the ship, the last thing I wanted was a girlfriend. I was determined to stay away from her."

"What happened?"

"She was acting squirrelly. She kept following one of the guests around. Finally, even though she didn't want to, she told me what was going on."

"About the death symbol?"

"Yeah."

"Did you believe her?"

Quinn worked his jaw as he debated how to answer. "I believed she believed it," he said finally. "I don't know what I believed. I could see the symbol when she pointed it out. I thought maybe it was a self-fulfilling prophecy. Maybe she made me see it. Most other people didn't see the symbol unless she expressly traced it for them."

"It obviously worked out, though," Jack noted. "You guys seem tight."

"We're close. We've worked hard to build something."

"And yet you're worried," Jack surmised. "You're worried that her ability keeps changing, and you're wondering if you'll be able to help her the way she obviously needs to be helped. You love her, want to be her knight in shining armor, but you often feel out of your element."

Quinn didn't bother to hide his surprise. "How do you know that?"

"Because it's the exact way I feel about Ivy," Jack replied without hesitation. "There's something about her that makes me want to take care of her. She's a strong woman, so she often fights that. She comes to me, though, when she's upset and wants to talk things out. That's a good thing. Obviously Rowan is the same way with you."

"How do you know that?"

"Because she eavesdropped on us in this very bar," Jack answered. "She ran straight to you because she wasn't sure what to make of the information she heard."

"You're not going to hold that against her, are you?" Quinn was stern. "She didn't go out of her way to listen to your private conversation. It simply happened."

"I'm not going to hold anything against her." Jack opted for honesty. "She wasn't trying to hurt us. She was looking for answers. Besides, in some ways, she reminds me of Ivy."

"Except she's my woman," Quinn reminded him, causing Jack to smirk.

"You don't have to worry about that. My heart belongs to Ivy, and that's never going to change."

"I see that every time you look at her. It's pretty obvious."

"Right back at you." Jack scratched the side of his nose as he eyed his new partner in crime. "I want to help you with this. Before you shoot me down, keep in mind that Ivy isn't going to be able to back away. What happened when she got inside Emily Little's head last night shook her. If it happens again, I won't have a choice but to act."

"I get that." Quinn wasn't happy, but he understood where the other man was coming from. "She blames herself, doesn't she?"

"Unfortunately, yes. There was nothing we could've done. She had no idea what she was seeing."

"Rowan blames herself, too," Quinn admitted. "No omen ever showed up on Emily's photo. She thinks she somehow screwed things up to make that happen ... although she has no way of controlling what went down."

"Why wouldn't the omen show up on Emily's photograph?" Jack seamlessly slid into cop mode. "Do you have any theories on why that is?"

"One. If a murder is spur of the moment, no premeditation, sometimes the symbol doesn't show up."

"I guess that makes sense." Jack stroked his chin. "Where do you think we should point ourselves next? Two women are dead and the killer is clearly on this ship. That can't make you happy."

"It doesn't," Quinn agreed. "We have a bigger problem, though. We go to port in Nassau tomorrow."

"Why does that worry you?"

"Because a killer could disappear on that island, not return to the ship, and there wouldn't be a thing I could do about it."

"Oh." Realization dawned on Jack. "I guess that means we should probably figure this out before then, huh?"

"That would be best for all of us."

"Okay, let's put our heads together. We should take the people in the executive group one name at a time."

"I don't see a better way to approach things."

SIXTEEN

I vy and Rowan were much more relaxed by the time the men returned to the loft suite. Jack immediately made his way to his fiancée, gracing her with a kiss and a hug while whispering something that only she could hear. Whatever it was made her smile, and Quinn couldn't help but marvel at the way Jack handled the situation.

"And here I thought you guys might fight over you referring to her as your woman, Jack," he teased, his hand lightly moving over Rowan's back as he sat next to her.

"I'm used to him being a Neanderthal," Ivy replied, resting her head against Jack's shoulder as they got comfortable on the couch. "What have you guys been up to over the last few hours?"

"We've been watching the other members of the group," Quinn replied. "They're not exactly prostrate with grief given the fact that two of their members are dead."

"No one liked Margaret," Rowan reminded him. "She was extremely unpopular."

"And now she's the symbol of the group for better or worse," Ivy mused, her fingers moving to Jack's hand so she could flip it over and trace his lifeline. "She's become a martyr for the cause, which makes her a lot more useful in death than she was in life."

Intrigued by the way she phrased it, Quinn leaned forward. "What do you mean?"

"Jack told me what the people he talked to said. None of them liked Margaret. She was gung-ho at the start but turned into something of an attention whore. That couldn't have sat well with the others who were there from the beginning."

"That's an interesting point," Quinn mused. "Brenda Farmer and Joseph Guthrie were there from the start, but they didn't get the attention that Margaret did. She was the self-appointed leader who got all the attention. The others were shoved to the side."

"Are they your prime suspects?" Jack asked.

"I don't know that I have prime suspects They're definitely interesting. I have a friend pulling background on them. In fact, I should check my email. He probably sent dossiers on both while we were distracted by ... magic talk."

Jack smirked. "Why don't you check your email in your office and then bring whatever you find back here? We can all go through the information together."

"Why don't I just use your computer?" Quinn shot back. "Or is there something there you don't want me to see?"

"I didn't bring a computer."

"Oh." Quinn was momentarily taken aback. "How can you travel without a computer?"

"We're on vacation."

"Besides, we're not really computer people in real life," Ivy added. "We spend most of our time outdoors. Jack uses a computer for work but rarely gets it out at home."

"I think we can make that work." Rowan got to her feet. "I'll go with you to get the information, Quinn, and we'll be back in about twenty minutes or so."

Quinn was confused. "Why can't you just wait here with them, Ro?"

Rowan blew out a heavy sigh. She'd done her best to be patient, but Quinn clearly refused to see what was right in front of him. "Because Ivy and Jack would like a few minutes alone to talk about things. Jack is worried about how things went and wants to make sure Ivy is comfortable going forward as a group."

"Oh." Quinn pressed his lips together, uncertain. "Am I supposed to be talking to you about the same thing?"

Jack barked out a laugh, genuinely amused. "You're funny, man. I thought I was lost in the relationship game until I met you. You make me look like a genius."

"Says the guy who refers to his fiancée as 'my woman,'" Quinn grumbled under his breath. "Fine." He held up his hands in capitulation. "We'll go and check my email, give you guys twenty minutes to grope in private, and then be back to come up with a plan of attack. Does that work for everybody?"

Rowan grabbed his hand, amused. "You'll have plenty of time to grope me, too. Don't worry."

Quinn's expression softened. "Finally something I want to do."

JACK WAITED UNTIL Quinn and Rowan were through the door to ask the obvious question.

"Are you okay? How did things go?"

Ivy, feeling more relaxed than she had in almost twenty-four hours, smiled. "It's okay. We spent most of our time talking about how we discovered we could do different things. I like her. I'm more worried about you and Quinn. You don't exactly play well together."

"Don't worry about us." Jack's fingers were gentle as they slid a strand of hair behind her ear. "We're working things out. We're not exactly buddies, but we both want what's best for you and Rowan. We both want to solve this. We're not going to start throwing punches or anything. You don't have to worry about that."

"Do you want to know what I think?"

"Always."

"I think you do like him. This is just your way of interacting. You're the same with Max. Maybe Quinn can be like another brother you never wanted."

"Oh, see, that's where you're wrong." Jack wrapped his arms around her and pressed a kiss to the corner of her mouth. "I would gladly trade my sister for Quinn or Max."

"You can't have Max. I need him."

"Fair enough." He briefly lowered his forehead to hers and sighed as he swayed back and forth. "We're going to figure this out, honey. I promise. I'll be with you the entire time."

"This isn't exactly how we planned for our vacation to go. I'm sorry."

"It's okay." Jack was matter-of-fact. "We're together. That makes this the best vacation I've ever been on."

"Me, too."

"This is only the beginning, Ivy. We're going to spend our lives going on vacations together. I'll make sure of it. We'll have plenty of chances to improve on the original."

"I'm still glad we did this. Even though we're dealing with murder — as usual — we've spent a lot of quality time together. I don't take it for granted."

"I don't either. I love you."

"I love you, too."

QUINN WAS STILL ANNOYED as he sat at his desk and checked his email.

"Fred came through. I have two files here to print out."

"Make two copies," Rowan suggested as she paced the area in front of Quinn's desk. "That will allow everyone to read through the information. It will be easier."

"I don't understand why I have to make things easier for them," Quinn grumbled.

"Because you're a good guy and know they have help to offer."

"Oh, *that*." Quinn rolled his eyes but hit the button to print two copies. As the machine sprang to life, he turned his full attention on Rowan. "Did things go okay on your end? Ivy seemed more relaxed when we returned."

"She's nervous about a stranger knowing her secret," Rowan replied. "I don't blame her. You have no idea how terrifying that is."

"You told me," Quinn pointed out. "You could've lied and kept me in the dark, but you took a chance and told me the truth. That worked out pretty well, if you ask me. I think it will work out for Ivy, too."

"It's still terrifying. Plus, that's different. I felt drawn to you from the start."

Quinn's lips curved. "I felt that way about you, too."

"I guess I'm saying that I instinctively trusted you. Ivy doesn't have that luxury. She's not wildly attracted to you. Jack knows her secret because she trusts him. It's not necessarily a bad thing to worry about who you tell your secret to."

"I agree wholeheartedly." Quinn slipped his arm around Rowan's waist and tipped her into his lap, pressing a light kiss to the tender spot behind her ear. "I don't think telling random people what you can do is a good idea. At all. However, life is about love and trust. If you find people you can trust, you should be able to be yourself with them."

"Ivy's life was different from mine, though," Rowan explained. "She grew up in a small town. St. Clair Shores wasn't exactly huge, but it was in a metropolitan area. I could disappear if I needed a break, or to hide. Shadow Lake was too small for Ivy to hide. Everyone knows everyone there."

"What are you saying?"

"She was always the odd one in town. Shadow Lake has one stoplight. Her best friend before Jack entered the picture was her brother. She doesn't have a lot of other friends."

Quinn smoothed Rowan's hair as he considered what she said. "I didn't really think about that. It kind of makes sense."

"Yeah. She's leery for a reason. I think she trusts me, although it's not easy for her."

"So it's just me that she doesn't trust."

"I don't know that I would phrase it that way," Rowan hedged. "She trusts Jack with her whole heart, though. I think that was probably a good choice because he loves her beyond reason."

"He certainly does," Quinn agreed. "He handles her well. That whole 'my woman' thing was a way to distract her from worrying about what would happen now that we know her secret."

"I picked up on that. He's not the type to think about her as property."

"They fit together." Quinn tightened his grip on Rowan's waist. "We fit together, too. I think we're going to be able to come to a meeting of the minds, all of us working together and thinking things through."

"I do, too."

"If Ivy doesn't trust me, it's okay. She trusts you and you trust me."

"I think it would be easier if you and Jack could at least pretend to like one another."

"I didn't say I disliked him."

Rowan made a face. "You guys are one bad testosterone frenzy away from thumping your chests and declaring yourselves king of the cruise ship."

Quinn smiled at the visual. "I would win that competition."

"See!" Rowan waved a finger in his face. "That's exactly what I'm talking about. Why are you guys acting this way?"

Quinn shrugged, noncommittal. "I don't know. It seems to come naturally for both of us."

"Well, knock it off. I don't think Ivy being on this particular cruise is a coincidence. I happen to believe in destiny. She's here for a reason."

"And what reason is that?"

"She's going to work with us — her and Jack — to help figure out what's going on with this group. That means we need her. You're going to have to find a way to get along with Jack if we expect this to work out the way we want."

"I don't dislike Jack," Quinn stressed. "In fact ... I kind of like him."

"You do not."

"I do, too. It's just ... I like him best when we're sparring. I don't know how to explain it."

Rowan tilted her head so she could stare into Quinn's eyes. "This is some weird man thing, isn't it?"

"Pretty much."

"Well, be careful that your sparring doesn't turn into punching. That's the last thing we need."

"Yes, ma'am." His smile was devilish as he lowered his mouth to Rowan's. "We have ten minutes before we have to go back. I have an idea how we can fill that time."

Rowan sighed. "Okay. This isn't doing anything to fix your gender's reputation as Neanderthal men, though."

"I can live with that."

TWO HOURS OF READING THROUGH boring files meant Ivy and Rowan worked up an appetite. Since Quinn and Jack were always up for a good meal, they headed to the dining room together.

Rowan and Ivy went through the line first, filling their plates. Jack was happy to see that Ivy's appetite appeared to have returned, which was a great relief to him.

"You need a better poker face," Quinn said as he moved to Jack's side, an empty plate in his hand. "It's okay to worry. You don't want her to know you're worrying, though. That will simply make her antsy."

Jack rolled his eyes as he grabbed a roll from the basket and dropped it on his plate. "Since when are you a relationship guru?"

"Um ... since always. I could give classes on relationships."

Jack snorted. "Now I know you're talking just to hear yourself talk. You're as clueless as me when it comes to relationships."

Quinn wanted to argue the point, but Jack wasn't wrong. "No matter what, I'm smarter than you. I'm simply not a genius when it comes to relationships."

"No one is." Jack's eyes remained on Ivy. "At least she's eating. She really hasn't eaten anything substantial since lunch yesterday. She was too worked up to eat the room service I ordered last night and she pushed both breakfast and lunch around her plate without really digesting anything."

"Do you constantly worry over her eating habits?"

"Not usually." Jack added huge mounds of shellfish to his plate as he watched Ivy scoop up a big serving of pasta. "She's a healthy eater, despite being a vegetarian. She's a marvelous cook."

"Except for those mushrooms you don't like."

"They taste like feet," Jack deadpanned. "She loves them, though.

She makes soup with them. She spends three straight weeks lost in the woods with her brother so they can pick as many of those stupid things as possible."

"It sounds like it's an interactive food affair."

"That's a good way of looking at it. I think they're gross, but she was hunting for morels right after we met. It's kind of an anniversary thing now. I went with her to hunt them this year, although I draw the line at eating them."

"It seems like a weird thing to me, but if it makes her happy, I don't see the harm."

"There's no harm." Jack forced a smile. "If I had a way to get those mushrooms for her right now I would actually eat the stupid things just to get a smile out of her. She had me worried for a little bit."

"Because she saw Emily Little's death?"

"Yeah. That's never happened before, at least like that. She's seen through the eyes of a killer before. I thought that was the worst thing ever. I was wrong. This was worse. She felt Emily's fear ... and I don't ever want her to be afraid."

"Right." Quinn's mind drifted as he filled his plate.

"You seem distracted," Jack said after a beat. "What are you thinking about?"

"You said she has magic dreams."

Jack glanced around to make sure nobody was listening and scowled. "Shh."

Quinn rolled his eyes. "No one cares what we're talking about. Most of them probably think we're together because we're so intense."

Jack snorted. "Dude, I so wouldn't date you if I rolled that way. You're too bossy."

"You like your women bossy."

"One woman. I like Ivy bossy." Jack smiled fondly as he watched his fiancée cross the room and sit at a table with Rowan. "She seems to be doing better."

"Yes, and I'm glad for that." Quinn meant it. "The thing is, you said she can do weird stuff in her dreams, go places."

Jack was instantly alert. "What are you getting at?"

"Hear me out."

"I already don't like whatever you're going to say."

Quinn chuckled, genuinely amused at Jack's reaction. "She's been in Emily Little's head. She saw what happened."

"And I'm not asking her to go back there." Jack was firm. "Get that notion out of your head right now."

"It wouldn't be real for her, though," Quinn persisted. "She could see what went down without being in any danger. That's like the perfect ability. She's a witness who can't be hurt because she's not really there."

"No." Jack vehemently shook his head. "I won't do that to her. She was inside Emily's head. That means she was the victim. If you think I'm putting her through that a second time, you're crazy."

"Maybe she can control her environment and look at the scene from a different angle."

"And if she can't, she's trapped."

"Yes, but that doesn't mean she's alone," Quinn pointed out. "You can go into the dreams with her. You can protect her."

Jack opened his mouth to argue and then snapped it shut. He was honestly intrigued by the suggestion. "I don't know," he said finally. "I have to think about it."

"Think about it." Quinn was unnaturally bright. "I think this is a great idea."

"That's because it's not your girlfriend. Would you be so geeked to try it if Rowan was the one who could get hurt?"

"No. The thing is, she would want to do it anyway because that's who she is. I think Ivy is the same way."

"And I think Ivy is the love of my life and I will not purposely hurt her for anything."

"Don't hurt her. Go with her."

Jack sighed. "I said I would think about it. Don't push me to make a decision before I'm ready."

"Fair enough." Quinn finished filling his plate with food. "Just out of curiosity, do you want to beat your chest and declare yourself king of the cruise ship?"

"Is that a real question?"

"It's something Rowan said."

"Well, I don't want to beat my chest. You, on the other hand, are a different story."

"You're not exactly a barrel of monkeys either."

"I'm more fun than you."

"In your dreams."

SEVENTEEN

The foursome spent their dinner hour watching the political group's main players and trying to get a feel for the dynamics of the group.

"If you ask me, Guthrie is trying to take over," Jack noted as he leaned back in his chair and wiped the corners of his mouth with his napkin.

"Why do you think that?" Rowan asked.

"Because he took the chair at the head of the table," Quinn answered.

"I believe she was asking me," Jack muttered.

"Oh, geez." Ivy rolled her eyes. "Why do you guys feel the need to fight? There's no reason for it."

"We're not fighting, honey," Jack replied. "This is simply the way we communicate."

"Well, it's stupid."

"I agree." Rowan scorched Quinn with a pointed look. "Knock it off. Go back to why Guthrie is trying to take over. All I see is a guy holding court in front of nine other people."

"Yes, but should he be holding court?" Quinn challenged. "At least on the surface, he should fake feeling sad over Margaret's death. None of those people look sad."

"Perhaps it's because Margaret was an unlikeable person," Rowan suggested. "No one I spoke with thought much of her."

"Which makes me wonder why they didn't try to usurp her power before this," Ivy mused. "The group has been in existence a couple of years, right?"

"It started with the three of them in a local fellowship group," Quinn explained. "It grew from there."

"And took over the church," Jack added. "Maybe someone at the church didn't like attention shifted from a message of faith to one of attack."

"I can see that," Ivy said, wiping her hands before reaching for her iced tea. "That would mean it's a person of faith doing the killing, though."

"Or a person hiding behind faith," Rowan corrected. "Most people of faith, those who truly believe, are good people. Sure, every once in a while a bad egg gets into the carton, but that's honestly the exception rather than the rule."

"I'm still leaning toward the possibility that someone joined the group late in the game so he or she could get close to Adkins," Quinn supplied. "Maybe it's not one of the executive group members."

"I thought you said that was unlikely given the fact that the cameras were shut down," Rowan countered.

"I still don't know why that request was made," Quinn admitted. "I've asked around. Margaret made the request. Whether she thought it was a good idea or someone else asked her to do it, though, I have no idea. The only one who might know who made that request is Emily, and she's dead, too."

"She's the one I don't understand," Ivy said. "She was basically a secretary. She had no power. Why kill her?"

"Because she knew something," Jack answered. "Or, even if she didn't know something, perhaps our killer thought she did."

"Do you think Guthrie is the likeliest suspect?"

"I don't know." Jack rested his hand on Ivy's knee under the table and gave it a reassuring squeeze. "He's a likely suspect. There's no getting around that. When I talked to Brenda Farmer, though, she wasn't a fan of Margaret's desire to take over the world either. She thought things should be more equal."

"She could be a suspect, too," Quinn said. "In fact, I have to think Margaret would've been more likely to allow Farmer into her room than Guthrie after hours. It might be sexist thinking, but it seems to me that Margaret's crusade for family values wouldn't allow her to invite a man into her room so late at night."

"Unless something was going on between them," Jack countered, digging through the files they'd brought with them to peruse over dinner. "Your friend said that Guthrie was checking into a hotel once a week to spend the night even though he owns a house."

"He's married," Rowan pointed out. "Why wouldn't his wife put up a fight about that?"

"Maybe she's having her own affair," Ivy interjected. "Or maybe he's bad in bed and has a rotten personality so she's simply happy to have a break from him."

"Your sunny outlook on life never ceases to entertain, honey." Jack tapped the end of her nose. "You should have some dessert, by the way. Make sure you're nice and full before we head back to the room for bed."

Ivy was caught off guard by the conversational shift. "Are you trying to fatten me up?"

"No. I wouldn't mind a smile, though. They have turtle cheesecake up there."

Ivy brightened considerably. "They do? I'll be right back."

Jack watched her go, a small smile playing at the corners of his lips. As soon as he was certain she was out of earshot, he pinned Quinn with a serious look. "I know what you're going to do. You're trying to find a roundabout way to suggest that the only true way to know who killed Emily is for Ivy to try and find her in a dream. I already told you I'm not comfortable with that."

Quinn adopted an innocent expression. "Did I insinuate I was going to do that?"

"Yes."

"When?"

"When we were in line getting food."

"I think you hear what you want to hear," Quinn shot back. "I agreed to let you think about things. I meant it. I've given it more thought and you're right, if Rowan was the one being asked to do this, I'm not sure I would be okay with it."

"Okay with what?" Rowan furrowed her brow, confused. "What are you guys talking about?"

"I may have suggested we ask Ivy to find out what happened to Emily in a dream," Quinn admitted, sheepish. "She's got that ability for a reason. I thought it might be a good time to use it."

"She's never been trapped in the part of victim before," Rowan argued. "That's not fair to her."

"That's what I said," Jack supplied. "I don't want her terrorized."

"I don't want to terrorize her either," Quinn said. "You're the one who told me you share dreams. You said you can direct them. I don't understand why you guys can't go in together. Then you can protect her."

"Can you do that?" Rowan was legitimately intrigued. "Can you stand with her in a dream?"

"We've never tried what your boyfriend is suggesting," Jack replied, bristling. "Our dreams are meant to be fun. We go to the beach ... and camping, which is something she likes and I tolerate. We have romantic picnics. We do not go to dangerous places to see if she can turn into Wonder Woman."

"I believe she's already Wonder Woman in your head," Quinn pointed out. "You believe she can do anything."

"She can."

"So why not ask her to do this?"

"Because I won't risk her for anything," Jack fired back. "She deserves a chance to rest and relax. This is supposed to be our vacation, for crying out loud."

"A vacation you interrupted to investigate a murder before she even had the vision."

"But ... ." Jack was frustrated, mostly with himself. "I'm not going to ask her to do it. You can't make me. And if you ask her, we really are going to do that chest thumping thing you mentioned in the buffet line. Don't push her to do something uncomfortable. I don't like it."

"I think it's already too late for that," Rowan said, inclining her head to the spot behind Jack, where Ivy stood with a huge piece of cheesecake.

"Honey ... ." Jack moved to stand, but Ivy shook her head.

"I want to hear Quinn's idea," she said as she reclaimed her chair. "If I understand correctly, you want me to force myself to go back into the memory, treat it how Jack and I do dreams, and try to come up with a face for the killer."

"You don't have to do it," Jack said quickly.

Ivy ignored him and remained focused on Quinn. "That's what you want, right?"

Now that he was staring into the fathomless depths of Ivy's eyes, Quinn wasn't sure how to respond. Finally, he opted to stick to the truth. "I think it's worth a shot."

"And what if it doesn't work?"

"Then at least we'll know."

Ivy sliced into her cheesecake and took a large bite as she mulled the idea. Jack watched her, concerned, and occasionally glared at Quinn for good measure. When Ivy was done chewing and swallowing, she slid a sidelong look to Jack.

"I'm guessing you don't like this idea," she said finally.

"I don't like anything that makes you upset."

"Yeah, well ... I don't see where we have a lot of choice in this matter."

Jack sighed, resigned. He could tell she meant business. If he wanted to change her mind, they would have to fight. He wasn't keen on that idea. "I'm going with you. I won't let you do this alone."

"I know." Ivy patted his hand before slicing off another huge bite of cake and holding her fork near Jack's mouth. "We're better when we do everything together."

Jack accepted the bite and stared at her as he swallowed. "I want you to pull the plug if things get too intense. Promise me."

"I promise."

"Fine." He rested his hand on top of hers. "We'll do it together."

"See, I told you this would work out." Quinn preened. "I was right and you were wrong."

"It hasn't worked out yet," Jack reminded him.

"When it does, I want you to thank me."

"You'll be lucky if I don't kick you."

"I'll consider that a win, too."

IVY SLIPPED UNDER SURPRISINGLY fast, leaving Jack behind to give chase. He rested next to her in bed, his tall frame pressed next to her slighter one, and willed himself to follow. His frustration was overwhelming when sleep refused to claim him. Settled in a crook of his arm, her head on his chest, Ivy lightly slumbered. Jack was left with nothing to do but force himself to calm, draw in deep breaths, and search for a way to follow.

He didn't want her to go through this alone.

In the dream, Ivy found herself on the deck of The Bounding Storm. The sky over the ocean was littered with clouds, lightning illuminating the heavens as she stared out at nothing but the vast expanse of water. She was alone, Jack still searching for a way to join her, but she wasn't afraid.

She knew that's what Jack worried about most, that she would be overwhelmed with fear and he wouldn't be near to offer comfort. He was smart, handsome, and unbelievably funny. Jack's biggest gift, though, was the way he made her feel. She never knew true comfort before him, and she didn't want to face a world where she had to go without it again.

"Nice night, huh?" The bartender was behind the counter. *Demarcus.* That was his name. He looked real, but Ivy was fairly certain he was a figment of her imagination.

"It's an interesting night," Ivy replied, choosing her words carefully as she sat on a stool. "What are you doing here? Were you here the night it happened?"

"I'm always here."

He was cryptic, causing Ivy to double down on her assumption that he was only present so she could have someone to bounce ideas off of.

"You haven't seen Jack, have you?"

"Your boyfriend? No. He's close but having trouble following."

"Why? He's never had trouble before."

"He's worked up, antsy. He can't slip under and join the dream. He's unbelievably frustrated. If you reach out with your feelings, you'll recognize that yourself."

Ivy knit her eyebrows and tilted her head to the side, thunder echoing throughout the night and causing her to straighten in her seat. "Jack's fueling the storm."

"Maybe," Demarcus said. "Maybe we're all fueling the storm. It's an existential question."

"Huh. I wonder why I made you talk like a weird philosopher. Maybe I needed the comic relief."

Demarcus winked. "What makes you think you're in charge of my personality?"

"Because you're not really here."

"Are you sure about that?"

Ivy wasn't sure of anything. Still, she turned to face the deck. "Emily Little was down that way when she was killed. Did you hear something that night? Probably not. You strike me as the type who would run to the rescue if you heard a scream. That means the storm either drowned out the noise or she didn't make any."

"The storm was fierce," Demarcus offered. "It was loud and strong, enough to kill the power."

"Unless something else killed the power, like a person."

"The odds of that are slim. Our security is very good."

"So, basically you're saying whoever killed Emily took advantage of the power outage," Ivy mused, taking a step away from the bar as she tapped her bottom lip. The deck remained illuminated, which meant the electrical failure was still to come. "Perhaps they were talking, arguing even. Emily let slip that she knew something. The killer was upset, worried he would be exposed.

"Then the power went out and he had exactly one chance to get rid of her without anyone seeing," she continued. "It must have seemed like divine intervention."

"It's coming soon," Demarcus supplied, taking Ivy by surprise when he handed her a flashlight. "You're going to need this."

"Emily didn't have a flashlight."

"You're not Emily."

"No, but I'm limited by what she saw that night," Ivy pointed out. "I can't see what she didn't see because I'm working from her memories."

"No, you're working with magic," Demarcus corrected. "Your fear keeps you from seeing how powerful you really are. You might want to look harder, put more effort in. The results could be interesting."

Ivy flicked on the flashlight at the exact moment the power went out on the ship. Even though she knew it wasn't real, a gasp lodged in her throat and she briefly pressed her eyes shut. When she opened them again, she found herself in a surreal world where the flashlight offered more light than should be possible.

"What the … ?"

Ivy didn't get a chance to dwell on her surroundings, or what Demarcus's appearance meant. The sound of voices on the deck assailed her ears, and when she turned back to invite Demarcus for a walk, he was gone. He wasn't real — she knew that — but racing to watch a murder would've been easier if she wasn't alone.

Still, Ivy steeled herself and broke into a jog, putting one foot in front of the other as she hurried toward the spot where Emily Little died. When she arrived, she focused first on the terrified woman backing toward the deck railing. Tears streamed down her face as the rain plastered her hair to her head.

"I can't believe you're doing this," Emily whined to no one in particular. However hard Ivy looked, she couldn't find anyone else to focus on. Emily appeared to be alone. "You're supposed to want to protect the world, not hurt it."

No one answered.

"Please don't do this," Emily begged. "I didn't know. I had no idea what was going on. I … just wanted to be part of something. I wanted to be part of this."

Again, no answer.

"Please don't do this!" Emily practically screeched her angst. "I don't want to die. I'll go away and never say anything about all of you, what you're doing. I promise."

All of you? Ivy sucked in a breath and looked around the deck again, trying to force herself to see faces. She couldn't, but slowly, several shapes started taking form.

She didn't recognize faces. It was more blobs than figures. She couldn't tell if she was dealing with men or women, or a mixture of both. She could count, though, and there were five shapes on the deck staring down Emily, closing the distance to the frightened woman.

"I'll forget what I saw, what I know," Emily offered. "You have my word. I'll be done with it all."

"It's too late for that," a voice rasped. It was neither male nor female, just ominous. "You should have thought about that before you got involved. We warned you. You didn't listen. You let ambition rule you. Now something else will rule you."

Ivy jerked her head away when the biggest shadow advanced on Emily and grabbed her by the neck. She pressed her eyes shut and put her hands to her ears to block out the noise. She wanted to wake up. She wanted to be anywhere other than here.

Then, suddenly, a hand rested on her shoulder and she viciously slapped out as she tried to stumble away from whoever dared pull her into the action. She moved so fast she tripped over her own feet and hit the deck hard enough that, even in a dream, her hip ached.

"Honey, it's me," Jack said quickly, dropping to his knees as he scrambled after her.

"Jack?" Ivy held back tears, but just barely. "You're here."

"Of course I'm here." He held open his arms. "I'm so sorry I didn't get here quicker. I couldn't fall asleep."

"It's because you were worried about me."

"Always."

Ivy launched herself into his arms and pressed her face to the hollow between his shoulder and neck. "It was more than one person, Jack. There were five of them. I think it might be at least half the members of the executive group. She begged for mercy, but they didn't listen."

"It's okay." Jack rubbed her back as he kissed her forehead. "It's okay. Did you see faces?"

"No. Just shadows."

"You're okay." Jack sat on the deck and tugged her until she was on his lap. "I won't let anyone hurt you. Not here. Not home. Not anywhere."

"I know. I was afraid when I couldn't find you."

"I'm sorry."

"It's not your fault. I faced it myself, though. I was strong."

"Oh, honey. You're the strongest person I know. I have you now, though. I'm not going anywhere. Not ever."

"I'm thankful for that."

"We both are."

18

EIGHTEEN

Ivy woke to find herself wrapped around Jack, her face pressed against his chest and their legs twined together. He was already conscious, his dark eyes on her. When she smiled, he returned it and pressed a soft kiss to her mouth before they could even share a word.

"Are you okay?"

Ivy nodded. "I am. Are you okay?"

"I wasn't the one left alone."

"I was never in danger."

"That's not how it felt."

Despite herself, Ivy chuckled. "I think you have a hero complex."

"I think I love you." Jack was in no hurry to untangle their limbs. "We need to talk about what you saw in the dream. You know that, right?"

Ivy nodded, solemn. "Yeah. We need to tell Quinn and Rowan."

Jack scowled. "I'm still angry he tricked you into doing what you did."

"It's only a trick if I don't know what I'm doing."

"Yeah, well, I still don't like it."

Ivy's sigh was long and pronounced. "Do you want to know what I think?"

"Most of the time. In this particular case, probably not."

"I think you and Quinn are a lot alike, which means your personalities naturally clash."

"I think I'm nothing like him."

"No? From where I'm standing — er, laying — I think you're both stalwart ... and protective ... and a little schmaltzy. I think he loves Rowan the same way you love me, with a fierceness that can't be measured. I also think you're both a little sarcastic."

"And I think you're hungry." He kissed the tip of her nose. "We promised Quinn and Rowan we would meet them for breakfast. We should shower and get cleaned up if we expect to make it on time."

"We could probably save time — and conserve water — if we showered together."

Jack's eyes lit with mirth. "That's a fantastic idea."

"Yeah. One thing before then, though." Ivy pressed her palm flat against Jack's chest. "I love you, too."

"I know. I'm lovable."

Ivy giggled as he tickled her, squirming as he pressed kisses to her neck. "We're not in the shower yet."

"Think of it as a head start."

ROWAN AND QUINN WERE already seated when Jack and Ivy hit the dining room. Jack signaled they were going through the buffet line and would join them shortly – something Quinn nodded in agreement to – and then disappeared in the line of hungry guests.

Rowan slid her eyes to Quinn, curious. "Do you think she did what you asked?"

Quinn shrugged, uncertain. "I don't know. I'm guessing she at least tried. I think Jack probably stopped her."

"Why would he do that?"

"Because he wants to protect her."

"Would you do any differently for me?"

"No." Quinn smiled as he covered her hand with his. "If you were the one who could see things in dreams and he suggested you try to sniff out a murderer, I wouldn't be happy about it. Still, we're running at a deficit here. We need to figure out who we're dealing with ... and fast. We dock this afternoon and our killer could disappear and never be heard from again."

"Well, let's not jump to the worst possible conclusion before it happens," Rowan suggested. "Try to look on the bright side. We still have time."

"Not much."

"Time is time."

"Yeah, well ... ." Quinn offered her a lopsided smile. "Have I told you how pretty you look today?"

Rowan glanced down at her simple T-shirt and shorts. "I look the same as I always look."

"Pretty."

Her cheeks flushing with color, pleasure spreading through her chest, Rowan leaned closer. "You're really good at making me feel like the prettiest woman in the world. Have I told you that?"

"A few times." He pressed a soft kiss to the corner of her mouth. "I like hearing it, though."

"I like saying it. I also like telling you that I love you."

"I like hearing that, too." He gave her another kiss. "We're going to figure this out. I have faith. If we don't ... well, we'll deal with it then."

IVY AND JACK'S PLATES WERE heaping with enough food that Quinn could do nothing but arch an eyebrow as they settled across the table.

"What?" Jack's tone was challenging. "Do you have a problem with breakfast?"

Quinn shook his head. "No. Are you trying to stock up so you can hibernate or something?"

"Ha, ha." Jack bit into a slice of bacon. "The food is good, and I rarely get breakfast meat unless we go out. I'm taking advantage of the situation to bulk up."

Rowan snickered at Jack's enthusiasm. "I don't see how you live in a house without meat. I would like to be high-minded and quit eating meat, too — I love animals — but I don't think I'll ever make it to that point."

"It's not so hard once you dedicate yourself to the decision," Ivy said. "If I was vegan, I would probably feel differently. I tried going vegan for a few weeks, in fact, but it didn't go well. I like cheese and eggs too much."

"If you were vegan, we would need separate refrigerators," Jack supplied.

"I like how you would still make it work; you would simply need another appliance," Quinn noted, chuckling. "That's true love."

"It definitely is," Jack agreed, watching as Ivy heaped butter and syrup on her French toast. She was nervous but didn't want to show it. He could read her better than most and he hated the antsy energy fluttering around her now. "Make sure you bulk up, honey. I think it's going to be a long day."

Ivy smiled, but the expression didn't make it all the way to her eyes. "Right."

Quinn's gaze was pointed as it locked with Jack's more militant stare. "How was your evening?"

"If you're asking if Ivy did as you requested and tried to revisit what happened on the deck the night Emily Little died, you can rest easy."

"You went back?" Rowan was officially intrigued as she held her coffee mug. "How did it go?"

"It was ... different," Ivy replied, unease settling on her diminutive shoulders. "I essentially woke up in the tiki bar."

"Alone," Jack stressed. "I wasn't with her."

Guilt rolled through Quinn's stomach. "Why weren't you with her?"

"Because he couldn't fall asleep," Ivy answered for him. "He was too keyed up, frustrated. He got there toward the end, but it was late in the game."

"And she was already surrounded," Jack muttered.

"Surrounded?" Quinn's brow wrinkled. "I don't understand."

"It was weird," Ivy explained. "Your friend Demarcus was there at the start, talking to me. He seemed to know what was going on."

"Demarcus?" Rowan made a face. "But ... how? Are you saying he can dream walk, too?"

"I don't think so, although I guess it's always a possibility. I think I didn't want to be alone so I created someone to talk to. Demarcus is always in the tiki bar so I put him there again so I wouldn't be afraid."

Jack's jaw tightened as he moved his hand up and down her back. "Honey, maybe you should eat your breakfast first. We can talk about this later."

"No, I want to talk about it now," Ivy said. "It's important."

"What happened after you talked to Demarcus?" Quinn queried.

"He gave me a flashlight."

"Because?"

"Because it was dark and the blackout was coming. I thought it was a nice gesture."

Quinn had no idea what to make of that. "Okay, well ... um ... ."

"When the power went out, I knew where to go," Ivy said. "By the time I got down there, Emily wasn't alone. I wasn't inside her mind this time, which was a relief. I could see her, hear her. She was afraid and said she wouldn't say anything, that she would leave the group and nobody would be the wiser."

"Did you see the person who killed her?"

Ivy exchanged a weighted look with Jack. "That's the thing. It wasn't one person."

"There were five people there," Jack volunteered. "I showed up at the end and I counted five figures. Before you ask, we couldn't make out any of the faces. It was dark and even with the flashlight, the figures that approached Emily were shrouded. Maybe because Ivy is limited to what Emily saw that night."

"Or maybe the truth was too terrible for Emily to comprehend so she wasn't thinking as fast as she normally would've been under less tragic circumstances and that's all that registered in her memory," Ivy countered. "Maybe the truth was too terrible to grasp so she only absorbed what she could handle."

"That sounds ... awful," Rowan said, shaking her head. "If it was five people, though, what are we going to do?"

"We need to find out why someone would want to kill Margaret,"

Quinn said. "She's the key to all this. I think Emily was collateral damage because she either knew who killed Margaret or there was a reasonable assumption that she would figure it out."

"I get the feeling you're right," Ivy said. "Emily seemed to understand why she was dying. She tried to negotiate right up until the end."

"And she couldn't manage to do it," Quinn mused. "Still, five people, how are we going to figure out who those five people are?"

"I think that will be easier than it sounds," Jack suggested, catching the security chief off guard. "Demarcus said that Emily was drinking with people in a bar the night she died, right? You mentioned that, said they weren't mourning properly."

"I believe I said they weren't broken up by what happened," Quinn clarified. "You're basically right, though."

"Emily wasn't alone in that bar," Jack said. "She was with people. It makes sense that the people she was with — at least some of them — are the ones we're looking for."

"Oh." Realization dawned on Quinn and he wasn't happy that Jack came to the conclusion before he could. "Crap. That does make sense."

"I figured you have cameras there," Jack added. "We can go through the footage."

"We definitely can."

"What should we do?" Rowan asked. "You can't cut us out of this."

"No," Quinn agreed. "I was thinking that you guys could head up to the deck, watch that executive group, and take some photos. If someone else is in danger, you'll see. If someone is missing from that group, you'll know. We want to keep an eye on them, especially since we're docking in a few hours."

"What do you expect to find in that amount of time?" Ivy asked. "How do you plan on narrowing this down?"

"I don't know," Quinn answered honestly. "We have to start somewhere, though."

QUINN AND JACK EXCUSED themselves to the security chief's office right after breakfast. Jack left Ivy with a kiss and a promise that — no matter what — if the case wasn't solved by the time they docked in Nassau, they would return to their vacation and let it go. Ivy didn't believe him, but Jack was firm. He had no intention of letting their first true vacation together be derailed.

"How is Ivy really doing?" Quinn asked as he booted up his computer. "Is she okay?"

Jack eyed him for a long beat. He wanted to be mean, kick Quinn in the kidneys and tell him that he shouldn't have forced Ivy's hand. Instead, he merely shrugged.

"She's okay," he said finally. "She's strong."

"She's definitely strong."

"That's the first thing I noticed about her," Jack admitted, a small smile playing at the corners of his lips. "She was mouthy ... and opinionated ... and bossy ... and barefoot at a crime scene. The sun caused the pink in her hair to shine in a way that made it look as if she had a pink halo."

Quinn snorted. "I think you're carrying things a bit too far."

"Oh, I know. That's how I remember her, though. I wasn't looking for love and I got smacked over the head with it. She had enough strength at the beginning for both of us."

"I think you probably had strength, too. You just didn't realize it."

"Not the strength she did."

"Yeah, well, I'm sorry I asked her to go into the dream. I thought you would be with her. I wouldn't have asked if I knew she would be alone."

"She seemed fine, if a little confused, when I found her," Jack said. "She wasn't afraid. She's rarely afraid of anything. I was the one who was afraid when I saw how many figures were surrounding her."

"I find that interesting," Quinn agreed, focusing on his computer as the screen came to life. "I'm going to pull up the video feed from the Neptune that night. At least we'll be able to see who Emily was with. It makes sense that at least one or two of those people followed her to the deck."

"I'm pretty sure Guthrie is one of them."

"How?"

"It's a feeling I can't shake," Jack replied. "The way he stepped in and took over the leadership role. He acts as if he's been waiting for the opportunity for quite some time. As if he was somehow anointed.

"The thing is, when I was talking to Brenda Farmer, she made it sound like the original threesome was always supposed to be equal," he continued. "She wasn't sorry about Margaret's death, but she seemed ... puzzled. I think that's the best word to describe her reaction. She was puzzled by how everything went down."

"She could simply be a good actress," Quinn suggested, his eyes narrowing as he studied the footage. "Okay. Here we go."

"She could be a good actress," Jack agreed, moving behind Quinn's desk so he could watch the footage over his shoulder. "I've been fooled by good actors and actresses before."

"Like your partner?"

Jack nodded, his shoulders stiff. "I didn't see him for what he was until it was too late. I should have. The signs were all there. I was blind to it, though. That's one of the reasons I was determined to keep people at a distance when I moved to Shadow Lake. I thought it would be easy to segregate myself.

"I had grand plans to live on the river and spend all my free time fishing," he continued, smirking at the memory. "Then, on my second day in town, we got a call about a body in a ditch. When we pulled up, there was a woman standing there. She had her hands on her hips and her skirt billowed in the breeze and I remember thinking I didn't have the strength to stay away from her. Right from the start, I knew she would change things for me."

Instead of laughing at Jack, Quinn merely nodded. "Rowan and I met under different circumstances. I get what you're saying, though. I thought I wanted to be alone until I met her. Then I couldn't imagine being alone. Right from that first meeting I was hooked."

"I guess we're both a little schmaltzy, huh?" Jack smiled when he thought of what Ivy said to him in bed that morning. "We're kind of alike ... even though we don't want to admit it."

"We definitely don't want to admit it," Quinn agreed. "Here's the group that night. Both Guthrie and Farmer are with Emily, and they seem intent on talking to her."

Jack furrowed his brow as he studied the footage. "Who are these two women with them?"

"Um ... ." Quinn tugged the manifest from the corner of the desk and started checking thumbnail photos. "That is Bonnie Rigby and Lettie Sanders. They're assistants for Guthrie and Farmer."

"Which makes sense." Jack's mind was working fast. "Emily was probably close with Bonnie and Lettie because they were all assistants. They probably shared information."

"And maybe Bonnie and Lettie are the ones who told Guthrie and Farmer that Emily knew something," Quinn deduced. "You're right. That does make sense."

"There's another guy there, though," Jack said, pointing toward the figure at the far end of the bar. "Do we know who that is?"

"Um ... ." Quinn pursed his lips as he looked for a match on the manifest. "I'm not sure. I ... wait. Here he is. Richard Johnson. It says he's part of the executive committee, although I'm not sure what he does with the group. There are long biographies for everyone but him."

An alarm began dinging in the back of Jack's mind. "That sounds suspicious, doesn't it?"

"It really does." Quinn rolled his neck until it cracked. "Why would they keep his position with the group under wraps like that?"

"I guess it's possible he's simply a journeyman of sorts. Maybe he does multiple things and hasn't settled into a simple position yet."

"Or maybe it's something else," Quinn said. "Either way, we need to question these individuals. I'm thinking maybe we should do it in a group setting."

Jack was surprised by the suggestion. "What do you mean?"

"I'll call them all in, let them sit in the interrogation room together, make them sweat."

"And then what?"

"And then we'll question them about what we know, bluff, and hope one of them takes the bait."

"What happens if they don't take the bait?"

"I have no idea. We don't have a lot of time, though. It's the best idea I've got."

"Then we should probably see if we can make it work." Jack was resigned. "I want Ivy here for it, though. I know she doesn't have a law enforcement background, but she deserves to see this through to the end."

"I won't cut her out."

"Because Rowan will make you pay if you do?"

Quinn's smile was sheepish. "And a few other reasons. That's the main one, though."

"You might be surprised. They could see something we don't."

"That's what I'm counting on."

NINETEEN

Collecting the members of the group wasn't easy. Quinn sent his workers to do the deed, stressing that it was simply because they needed answers to fill out reports for the mainland police when they landed. Johnson and Guthrie put up the biggest fights, which was telling in Quinn's book. Still, he treated the men with a welcoming smile and profuse apologies.

"I'm really sorry about this," he started.

"Then perhaps you shouldn't be doing it," Guthrie suggested, his eyes filled with fire. "I'm pretty sure you don't have the authority to question us."

"Yes." Brenda Farmer bobbed her head. "Shouldn't we have lawyers for this?"

"That's certainly your choice," Quinn said. "If you feel you need an attorney, we have two on the ship to act as representatives."

"Attorneys that are on your payroll," Guthrie pointed out.

"True, but they work for their clients, which would be you in this particular case."

"So you say." Johnson was disgusted as he folded his arms over his chest. "I don't think I'm going to agree to this. You can't make me."

"You're right. I can't make you answer questions." Quinn's voice was smooth, earnest. "I can, however, lock you in a holding cell until we land back in Florida in three days if you don't choose to answer questions."

"That's the exact opposite of due process."

"And yet you agreed to those terms when you checked in." Anticipating trouble, Quinn had collected copies of their intake documents and provided Johnson the one he signed upon checking into his room. "If you look right there, you'll see what I'm talking about."

Johnson frowned as he read the document. "I don't remember agreeing to this."

"And yet you did."

Johnson's eyes were cold when he lifted them. "So, you're basically saying that you're going to lock us up if we don't answer your questions."

"I'm saying that we've had two murders since we left port and both are members of your group."

Farmer uncomfortably shifted from one foot to the other as she glanced between faces. "I don't understand why you picked the five of us, though. That doesn't make sense to me."

"You're one of the two leaders of the group now," Quinn pointed out. "Who else should be answering questions?"

"I ... ."

"As for your assistants, we have a separate room for them," Quinn barreled forward. "They'll be questioned by a different team."

Whatever Johnson was expecting, that wasn't it. "Why are you separating them?"

Quinn didn't answer, his smile enigmatic. "Are you ready to get started?"

ROWAN WAS THE ONE who suggested isolating the assistants. The idea came to her shortly before the security guards tracked down the necessary group members. She figured they were the least likely to have been involved in actual violence, perhaps feeling guilty because Emily was once a friend. Also, once they weren't under the thumbs of the bigwigs, they were more likely to talk.

"Can I get you some coffee?" Ivy asked, a carafe in her hand as she watched the young women settle at the conference room table. They looked confused and unsure of themselves.

"Just water," Bonnie replied, her voice raspy. "I don't need the caffeine. I'm jittery enough."

"I don't blame you." Rowan took the seat at the head of the table, enjoying her position as lead interrogator. "Emily was probably a friend of yours, right?"

Bonnie exchanged a quick look with Lettie before swallowing hard and nodding. "We spent a lot of time together because we were all assistants. We were supposed to coordinate our efforts so we never overlapped. That meant we met twice a week to schedule things."

"You must be broken up about her death," Ivy said. "I mean ... for her to die the way she did, running on the deck during a blackout, all of that darkness surrounding her, people she thought of as friends grouped together to end her life."

Bonnie balked. "What? How do you know that?" She realized what she said too late to take it back. "I mean ... what makes you think that happened?"

Rowan and Ivy were supposed to play it cool, warm up the girls and get them talking if they could while Jack and Quinn handled the bigwigs. Ivy was good at reading people, though, and she sensed a chink in the group's armor that she could exploit.

"We know everything that happened," Ivy lied, ignoring the side-long look Rowan lobbed in her direction and focusing her full attention on Bonnie. "We know that you were all drinking together at the Neptune Bar. We know that you were having a good time."

"I hardly think we were having a good time," Lettie interjected. "We were mourning a friend, drinking in her honor."

"A friend that was killed by the same people who killed Emily Little," Rowan pointed out.

"No, that's not true." Bonnie turned shrill. "That's not what happened at all."

"Shut up," Lettie snapped, her temper showing. "Why are you acting like an idiot? They don't know anything. They're simply trying to get you to admit you know something, which we don't because we weren't involved."

Lettie was smarter than Bonnie, but not by much, Ivy internally mused. They were both weak links. One good push would send them both over the edge.

"Let me tell you what I think happened," Ivy said, a plan forming. "I think you were in the Neptune having a few drinks, probably reminiscing about how horrible Margaret was and how nobody was sorry to see her dead. You could do that because everyone in your group hated Margaret and you didn't have to worry about offending anyone."

Lettie jutted out her lower lip. "That is not true."

Ivy ignored the denial. "At some point Emily let it slip that she knew who killed Margaret. She was always a loose thread you weren't sure you could keep from fraying. Heck, maybe she knew you were going to kill Margaret from the start and you were worried she couldn't keep her mouth shut. That's possible, right?"

"We didn't kill anyone." Bonnie sounded like a strangled mouse. "Stop saying that."

"Emily realized what was about to happen when it was too late to run," Ivy said. "You were in the hallway and the blackout occurred. Did you cause that, or was it simply a happy coincidence?"

"How would we cause that?"

"So ... a happy coincidence." Ivy already assumed that was the case, but she was happy for the confirmation. "Emily realized her fate in the hallway and she was desperate to get away. She ran, believing that if she found people on the deck that she would be okay. You couldn't hurt her with people present.

"Unfortunately for Emily, the deck was empty," she continued, losing herself in the memory of the event. "It was storming. People were inside. There were no lights because of the power outage. You had a perfect opening to kill Emily, so that's what you did."

"No!"

"Don't bother lying," Rowan interjected, a plan forming. "Even though the power was out, the cameras on the deck run on a backup generator. They're night-vision. We know what happened out there."

"But ... ." Bonnie made horrified chicken noises as she flapped her arms. "It wasn't our fault. We didn't want it to happen. Emily wouldn't keep her mouth shut, though. She knew what happened in Margaret's room, and even though she was part of the plan at the start, she decided she was going to confess when we got home. We couldn't have that."

Rowan leaned back in her chair, triumphant. "And who actually did the deed? Was it Johnson or Guthrie?"

"Does it matter?" Bonnie was morose. "We're all going to prison."

"Oh, it matters."

JACK STOOD IN THE FAR corner of the interrogation room, his arms folded over his chest. He was mildly amused at the setting, never having been in an interrogation room this clean before, but he was having a good time watching Johnson, Guthrie, and Farmer squirm like worms on the end of a hook.

"I don't know what you want us to say," Guthrie offered. "We don't know what happened to Margaret or Emily. If we knew, don't you think we would tell you?"

"I guess that depends," Quinn replied. "If you have something to lose by sharing the story, I can't see why you would volunteer any information."

"And what would we have to lose?" Guthrie was the picture of innocence, except for his eyes, which flashed with hatred and loathing. "Margaret was the face of our organization. Losing her is a blow. We don't benefit from that."

"Maybe not over the short term," Quinn agreed. "Over the long term, though, that's a different story. You're trying to point a finger at violence in the media. For Margaret to be taken down in a violent manner, that sort of makes her a martyr for the cause, doesn't it?"

"I ... ."

"Sure it does," Jack said hurriedly, cutting Guthrie off before he could comment. "She's going to be associated with your group forever. She'll always be the crusader who was cut down in her prime by a villain who only proved she was the right woman for the job."

Guthrie's lips curved down. "Margaret was a tireless promoter for the group. As sad as it is, she would be happy to know that her death meant something. She was a ... visionary ... as far as our group is concerned. She was a powerhouse."

"And that bothered you because you were supposed to be equals," Quinn noted. "You, Brenda, and Margaret founded the group together. At first, you didn't think much of it when she was the one getting interviewed by local newspapers. You had to take whatever publicity you could get.

"As the group started growing, though, and the message spread, bitterness became pervasive," he continued. "Margaret became the official face of the group, and that wasn't supposed to happen."

"So you think we killed her?" Guthrie challenged. "Don't you think that's a little extreme?"

"I think Margaret had an extreme personality," Quinn replied without hesitation. "I think she was hard to deal with and the more attention she got, the bigger her ego grew. I think she looked down on you and there became a point where it was intolerable."

"The cruise must have been a godsend," Jack added, his demeanor calm. "You couldn't attack her in a metropolitan area. Cameras are always an issue. I have to hand it to whoever suggested the cameras be turned off in your little corner of the ship, though. That was a masterful stroke."

"You should've thought about those cameras when you went after Emily Little, though," Quinn said.

"We didn't go after Emily Little," Farmer barked, her eyes wild. "How can you even suggest that? She was a young woman, a girl really, and she had her whole life ahead of her. Why would we go after her?"

"I can answer that," Ivy said, walking into the room without knocking. The ballsy move irritated Quinn, but not enough for him to interrupt her.

"Who are you?" Johnson asked, looking her up and down with a jaded eye. "I didn't realize ship security employed a woman with pink hair. I was already unimpressed with things given how many people have died under your supposed watch, but this is simply too much."

"Yes, my hair color is so much worse than murder," Ivy drawled, rolling her eyes.

"What did you find out?" Jack asked, hoping to steer the conversation in a different direction. "Did they admit to what happened?"

Ivy nodded. "They're being moved to holding cells right now. You were right about the power outage, Quinn. They didn't plan it. They simply took advantage of what happened. They didn't realize there were night-vision cameras on the deck that work on generator power."

It took Quinn a moment to realize what Ivy was saying, the lie she was doubling down on. He was impressed with her fortitude. "Yes, well, we were just about to get to the camera situation in here."

"What cameras?" For the first time since entering the room, Guthrie looked worried. He shifted on his seat and glanced to his left and right, obviously looking for support from Johnson and Farmer. Neither returned his gaze. "What cameras are you talking about?"

"There are cameras on the deck and they don't go down in case of a power outage," Quinn lied smoothly. "We saw what happened the night Emily Little was murdered."

"We know that you were the one who strangled her, Mr. Guthrie," Ivy added helpfully. "We also know that you're the one who killed Margaret in her room. She thought Mr. Johnson was coming for another special visit, a private one, but you showed up instead. He was supposed to do the deed – that's why he got close to her in the first place and had no specific job description in his biography – but he chickened out at the last minute. Since you were the one pushing for her death, you had to kill her. It turned out to be more fun than you expected, didn't it?"

Guthrie worked his jaw. "I think I need a lawyer."

"I think you do, too," Quinn said. "In fact ... ."

He didn't get a chance to finish what he was saying. Guthrie was on his feet, lightning quick, and he grabbed Ivy around the throat as he jerked her in front of him and pressed his back to the wall to make sure he couldn't get attacked from behind.

"Now you listen to me! I want off this ship right now. I'm not going to let you hold me. I'm not going to jail."

Jack, fury in his eyes, took two long strides toward Guthrie. He only stopped when the man gave Ivy a vicious shake and caused her eyes to go wide as her oxygen intake was cut off.

"I'm not kidding," Guthrie hissed. "I want off this ship. I was planning on running in Nassau anyway. I made arrangements. I realized after the fact that taking out Emily was a mistake, but it was too late. I couldn't change what happened."

"Why did you kill her?" Quinn asked, alarmed. The look on Jack's face told him the big man was going to launch himself at Guthrie to save Ivy. Since Ivy could get hurt in the process, Quinn was keen to keep that from happening. "Why not just let her go?"

"Because Emily couldn't take the guilt," Ivy volunteered, her anger on full display as she clawed at Guthrie's hand. "Stop touching me. I don't want you touching me."

"Shut up!" Guthrie gave her another violent shake. "You're my ticket out of here, for better or worse. I'm taking you with me. Once I get off the ship, once I'm safe and away, I'll let you go."

"Oh, whatever." Ivy was at the end of her rope. "No one believes that. You've murdered two women. You've got a taste for it now. You won't let me live because it's not in your nature. Oh, hey, maybe you've played too many video games."

"You've got a mouth on you." Guthrie squeezed Ivy's throat. "Don't push me, girl!"

"Let her go." Jack's voice was dark and dangerous as he stared Guthrie down. "I'll kill you with my bare hands if you don't."

"Oh, really?" Guthrie didn't look worried. "Have you ever done that? I have. It's not as easy as it sounds."

"It got easier the second time, though, didn't it?" Jack snapped. "You enjoyed it the second time. You're a sick bastard. As for what I'm capable of doing to you, you'd be surprised. If you hurt her, I swear, you're going to find out."

"He's not joking." Quinn tried one more time for calm. "He's a police officer from Detroit. They have different rules there. He'll take you out without thinking twice about it. Especially if you hurt her."

"And what does she have to do with him?"

"She's going to be my wife," Jack replied without hesitation. "She's already the love of my life. People have killed for less than love, but love is the greatest motivator out there. If you don't let her go right now, I will end you. I am not kidding."

Guthrie blinked several times in rapid succession, uncertain. "But ... how am I supposed to get off this ship without her?"

"That's not going to happen regardless," Quinn replied quietly. "We knew you were guilty when we brought you in. There's no getting out of here. The entire facility is being watched via closed-circuit cameras. There is no escape for you."

"But ... ." Guthrie was clearly having trouble accepting that simple fact. "This is not how it was supposed to go down."

"Well, not everything works out how you expect it to," Quinn said. "You need to release Ivy. If you don't, I won't be able to stop what's about to happen. Jack will kill you."

Guthrie gave Jack a long look, perhaps internally debating whether he could take the big man. Finally, he realized he wasn't strong enough to fight a trained police officer and he slowly released Ivy, giving her a disgusted shove in Jack's direction.

"Fine. Take her."

Jack caught Ivy with his left arm, pulling her close. With his right, he unleashed a nasty jab to Guthrie's face, causing the man to widen his eyes as he staggered to his side and dropped to his knees before sliding to the floor.

"Nice shot," Quinn noted as Jack buried his face in Ivy's hair. "It's going to be hell to explain to the authorities when we land, but it was a nice shot."

"I don't care about explaining it." Jack pulled back and stared into Ivy's eyes. "He had it coming. Are you okay, honey? Did he hurt you?"

Ivy's grin spread across her face quickly. "No. I'm fine. I got to interrogate people and make them cry. Those assistants were putty in my hands."

Jack laughed as he ran his hands over her back. "I'm glad you enjoyed yourself. What about your neck? Is your neck okay?"

"It's fine, although I may need a massage later."

"I'm happy to oblige."

"Somehow I knew you would say that." Ivy rolled to the balls of her feet and smacked a loud kiss against the corner of his mouth. "So, who wants lunch? I'm starving."

TWENTY

J ack and Ivy swung their linked fingers as they moved through the adorable Nassau market later that afternoon. Once the confessions were on record — some more tearful than others — Jack found he could easily let the investigation go. It was Quinn's domain, after all. Jack was on vacation, and he was determined to enjoy the last three days they had together.

"What about this?" Jack pointed toward a funky mask. "I think Max would love that."

Ivy insisted on picking up souvenirs for her loved ones, something Jack found adorable, and they'd spent the past two hours selecting things for her parents and his mother and sister. All that was left was her beloved brother, and she was having trouble finding something good enough.

"Why would I want to get him a mask?" Ivy asked, wrinkling her nose. "That's not very vacation-y."

Jack snickered. "Yes, but I think he should cover up that hideous face of his as often as possible."

"I'm going to tell him you said that."

"Go ahead." Jack took the mask off the rack and flipped it over, grinning when he read the back. "It's a fertility mask. It's supposed to make him more potent and desirable to women."

"Really?" Ivy was suddenly interested. "He would actually like that."

"He would," Jack agreed, grinning. "I think it's a winner."

"Okay." Ivy paid for the mask and added it to her haul, which included a necklace Jack insisted on buying her to mark the trip. She bought him a shell necklace in return, something she knew he wasn't overly keen about, but he agreed to wear it to make her happy. That was good enough for her. "We should get going. Do you know where the restaurant we're supposed to be meeting Quinn and Rowan is located?"

"Yeah. It's about three blocks that way." Jack pointed. "I'm hungry. This is good timing."

"You're always hungry."

"No, I'm always a fool in love for you. I'm only hungry half the time." He kissed the back of her neck as she giggled, happy when she tucked herself in at his side for the walk to the restaurant.

It only took them a few minutes to find the outdoor eatery, which was located on the water and absolutely gorgeous. Ivy was in love with the twinkle lights decorating the patio, and she waved when she caught sight of Rowan.

"They're already seated."

"Of course they are," Jack grumbled as he followed her toward the table. "Quinn needs to pick out the table. Otherwise he won't be able to eat because he won't feel in control."

Ivy slid him a sidelong look. "I thought you were over this competition thing with him."

"Who says we're in competition?"

"Anyone who has ever spent more than two seconds with you two in the same room."

"I think you're exaggerating, honey. I don't have a competitive bone in my body."

She snorted, genuinely amused. "Yeah. That's exactly what I think whenever you and Max decide to fight for couch superiority at our house."

"Hey, I live there now. I'm king of the couch."

"That's what I thought."

Rowan greeted them with a happy smile, helping Ivy with her bags as she settled and "oohing" and "aahing" over the souvenirs as Ivy opened a bag and gave her a gander of the treasures.

"What's with the fertility mask?" Quinn asked when Ivy held it up. "Are you guys planning for kids already?"

Jack shook his head. "No. We want to get married first, if my little honey bear will pick a date, that is."

Ivy's lips curved down. "Honey bear?"

"Oh, you don't like that." Jack's smile widened. "I'm going to keep calling you that until you set a date. I don't understand why it's such a big deal."

Honestly, Ivy didn't either. The idea of standing in front of people she trusted and cared about while declaring her love for Jack was exciting, not terrifying. It was the planning and shopping that went along with the event that gave her pause.

"You need to get me potential dates from your mother," Ivy said. "When is she open and available to come to Shadow Lake?"

"That's not how it works." Jack shook his head, firm. "We set the date and she arranges her schedule accordingly."

"I think he's right," Quinn noted. "That *is* how it works."

"Oh, that must have been hard for you to admit," Jack drawled. "The part about me being right, I mean."

Quinn rolled his eyes. "You're a real piece of work. Has anyone ever told you that?"

"No. Most people think I'm a joy to be around."

Quinn made a tsking sound with his tongue. "I have no idea how you put up with him, Ivy. You're a true delight and he's a ... butthead."

Ivy and Rowan laughed in unison, tickled.

"He's not so bad," Ivy said when she recovered. "After all, he did punch Joseph Guthrie in the face to defend me. Who doesn't love a strong protector?"

"He shouldn't have put his hands on you." Jack was still traumatized by the turn of events. "He's lucky I didn't rip his head off his shoulders."

"He would've had it coming," Quinn agreed. "By the way, after you guys left, everyone confessed their part in the plot. It seems they're already angling for deals."

"And what was the plot?" Ivy asked, smiling as the waitress delivered menus and glasses of water, promising to return and gather their orders in a few minutes. "Did they say why they killed Margaret? All Bonnie and Lettie would say is that she was insufferable and had to go."

"As far as I can tell, that's everybody's reason for doing it," Quinn replied. "Margaret essentially tortured them for years, fueled their jealousy, and they all got drunk one night and banded together to hatch a plan."

"What about Emily?" Jack queried. "Was she involved from the start, too?"

"No. They brought Emily in after the fact. They needed more access to Margaret. I guess, the bigger she got in her own head, the more she isolated herself from the others."

"I'm willing to bet that Margaret recognized the way the others felt about her," Rowan said. "She probably got off on it. She was having a fling with Richard Johnson, something he instigated because they needed more information from her. That's why he was part of the executive group."

"Yeah, that was something I didn't understand," Ivy admitted. "Why get involved with someone simply to kill her?"

"Margaret kept certain files to herself," Quinn replied. "She was the de facto head of the organization, so she simply had more information at her fingertips than everybody else. They wanted to get their hands on that information — especially the financial information — and they needed an inside man to do it.

"According to Johnson, he actually hated her and pretending he didn't was the hardest thing he's ever done," he continued. "He said she made his skin crawl and there were times he had to stop himself from smothering her with a pillow."

"You would think a woman who fancied herself a good judge of character would've figured that out," Ivy noted.

"Maybe she did see it," Rowan suggested. "Maybe she saw it but didn't care. It's lonely on the top. Even people like Margaret need loving sometimes."

"I guess." Ivy rubbed the back of her neck as she stared at the swirling ocean waters. "Did they even try to talk to Emily before killing her, or was Guthrie too far gone by then?"

"Guthrie has stopped talking and is claiming he has a mental defect," Quinn replied. "He's saying that he went temporarily insane and needs professional help. As for the others, Brenda Farmer is being the most helpful. She's not breaking down into tears every five seconds, and instead seems to be owning what she did.

"She doesn't deny that killing Margaret because she was stealing the limelight seems petty, but she's also not sorry it happened," he continued. "She's more upset about what happened to Emily. She says, seeing the way Guthrie snapped on the deck, that she was worried he would go after the rest of them eventually because the only way to keep his secret was to make sure nobody ever shared it.

"She said she was going to wait until they got home and then go to the police herself," he said. "I'm guessing she had plans to twist the story, make herself a scared victim, but it's too late for that now.

"On the night they killed her, she suggested that they give Emily a few days to calm down," he said. "She said it was simply nerves causing the girl to act out of sorts and if they all talked to her they could get her back to their way of thinking. That didn't happen."

"It's all unbelievably tragic because none of it had to happen," Ivy lamented, shaking her head. "It's kind of sad when you think about it. They thought they were going to change the world for the better and they all lost their heads and turned into the one thing they were fighting against."

"I'm going to guess a guy like Guthrie has been violent before," Jack offered. "He seems the type. He probably joined the group because it made him look like a good guy, served as decent cover, and allowed him to be as evil as he wanted to be while screaming from the rooftops that he was moral and just."

"Sadly, that's the feeling I get from him, too," Quinn agreed. "I don't think he's a good guy. I don't even think he's a middle-of-the-road guy. I think he's always been evil."

"What will happen to him now?" Ivy asked.

"They'll sit in holding until we get back to Florida and then they'll be taken into custody. I'm not sure what's going to happen to the other members of the group. They're going to notice when their leadership doesn't appear in the conference rooms they've booked for tomorrow. I guess we'll have to tackle that when it happens."

"Are you done with the case when the Florida cops take over?" Jack asked.

"I'll have to provide them with reports, maybe offer some testimony, but I'll pretty much be done. The confessions were recorded and those videos will be handed over, too. Believe it or not, this isn't the first time something like this has happened on The Bounding Storm."

"I guess living on a cruise ship is more exciting than I envisioned," Ivy said. "I'm just glad it's over. Jack and I still have three days of sun and fun to enjoy."

Jack pursed his lips as he brushed her hair away from her shoulder. "I'm sorry I got distracted. That wasn't fair to you."

"I knew what I was getting myself into when I took you on," Ivy pointed out. "You can't stop yourself from searching for answers, trying to protect those who might be in trouble. I wouldn't change that for anything. I'm pretty happy with my choice."

"Oh, so sweet." Jack gave her a kiss, grinning when he found Quinn glaring at him. "What?"

"Nothing. I'm just now realizing how schmaltzy and annoying Rowan and I must come across to others when we do the same thing."

"I like being schmaltzy," Rowan said. "It makes me feel warm all over."

"I'm going to make you feel warm all over when we get back to the ship," Quinn promised. "Our time together over the last few days hasn't exactly been quality time."

"And now I'm grossed out," Jack grumbled.

"You're fine." Ivy patted his knee under the table and rested her head against his shoulder. "Even though we took down a gang of murderers in the middle of everything, this is still the best vacation I've ever had."

"That's because it's the only vacation you've ever had."

"Still ... ." Ivy turned whimsical as she stared at the water. "We should walk along the beach at dark. I've never done that by the ocean."

"I think that can be arranged."

"You should definitely do that," Rowan enthused. "Quinn and I do that when we're docked in Florida all the time. In fact, that's part of our routine the night before departing. We walk on the beach and build sandcastles."

Jack snickered. "You make sandcastles, Quinn? That's so ... domestic."

Quinn scowled. "Please. You'll be making sandcastles before the night is out. The look on your girlfriend's face promises that."

Jack slid his eyes to Ivy and found her eyes sparkling. She was clearly in love with the idea. "I can live with that," he said finally. "We're on vacation. Whatever she wants goes."

Ivy's smile was so big it almost swallowed her entire face. "And don't you forget it."

CPSIA information can be obtained
at www.ICGtesting.com
Printed in the USA
FFHW021051291018
49068454-53335FF